"You're untemptable, right? Your absolute rejection of any physical intimacy is cowardly."

"In what way?" Antonio asked icily, his words sharply enunciated. "Doesn't it denote self-control?"

Something burned in his eyes now, but Bella was too hurt to take heed and too hurt to stop herself lashing out. "Maybe you're afraid that once you start, you won't be able to stop."

Silence strained for two beats before he broke it with a soft-spoken, hard-hitting whisper. "You want me to prove it?"

He didn't move a muscle, but somehow he made the room smaller. The subtlest change in his tone, the darkening in his eyes put her senses on alert. He'd gone from angered to something else altogether. Something more dangerous.

Goose bumps rose on her skin, but deep down, satisfaction flickered. "You don't have to prove anything to me."

He walked closer until he loomed in front of her. She held her ground and watched. *Dared.*

These powerful princes request your presence before

The Throne of San Felipe

Destined for the crown, tempted to rebel!

Crown prince Antonio and his wayward brother, Eduardo, have grown up in the shadow of the San Felipe throne. Now, with their royal destinies fast approaching, the rebel princes must choose their path.

They've always resisted expectation, so the kingdom waits with bated breath to discover if the San Felipe heirs will be dictated by duty, or ruled by desire...

Find out in:

The Secret That Shocked De Santis

The Mistress That Tamed De Santis

Available now from Harlequin Presents.

Natalie Anderson

THE MISTRESS THAT TAMED DE SANTIS

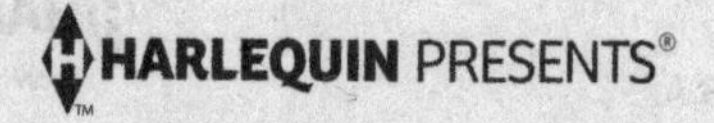

Recycling programs for this product may not exist in your area.

ISBN-13: 978-0-373-13947-7

The Mistress That Tamed De Santis

First North American publication 2016

This edition published by arrangement with Harlequin Books S.A.

For questions and comments about the quality of this book, please contact us at CustomerService@Harlequin.com.

Printed in U.S.A.

Natalie Anderson adores a happy ending—which is why she always reads the back of a book first. Just to be sure. So you can be sure you've got a happy ending in your hands right now—because she promises nothing less. Along with happy endings she loves peppermint-filled dark chocolate, pineapple juice and extremely long showers. Not to mention spending hours teasing her imaginary friends with dating dilemmas. She tends to torment them before eventually relenting and offering—you guessed it—a happy ending. She lives in Christchurch, New Zealand, with her gorgeous husband and four fabulous children.

If, like her, you love a happy ending, be sure to come and say hi at Facebook.com/authornataliea, follow @authornataliea on Twitter or visit her website/blog, natalie-anderson.com.

Books by Natalie Anderson

Tycoon's Terms of Engagement
Whose Bed Is It Anyway?
The Right Mr. Wrong
Blame It on the Bikini
Waking Up in the Wrong Bed
First Time Lucky?

The Throne of San Felipe

The Secret That Shocked De Santis

Visit the Author Profile page at Harlequin.com for more titles.

For my husband and family,
and for the laughter we share.

CHAPTER ONE

CROWN PRINCE ANTONIO DE SANTIS strolled along the dark street, savouring the stolen moment of freedom as he walked off the burn from the last eighty minutes in the palace gym.

Silence. Solitude. Darkness. Peace.

He checked the hood of his sweatshirt still hid most of his face. He'd soon have to turn back. In less than an hour this road would be crawling with workers frantically finishing preparations and testing the barricades they'd installed over the last day. The crowds would gather early too. San Felipe's car rally was prestigious, hotly contested and the starting gun for the annual carnival, which meant Antonio's next couple of weeks were even more packed than usual. State balls, trade meetings, society events, the carnival celebrations required a round-the-clock royal presence as the world's wealthy and glamorous came to indulge and experience his country's beauty. And with his younger brother away, Crown Prince Antonio was the only royalty on offer.

He'd do it all anyway; he always did.

He approached an intersection. The road to the left headed into the heart of the city and was the entertainment 'strip'—lined with restaurants and bars that would soon be packed for race action. He glanced up at the ornate exterior of the former firehouse on the corner—the latest building to have been reclaimed and refurbished into a hot night spot. But after only a week of business, the city's residents were debating the merits of this particular establishment more than any other.

BURN.

The four bronze letters bolted to the wall screamed both defiance and demand. He read it as a blatant statement of intent—she was here, she didn't care, and she didn't intend to hide.

Antonio frowned. Suddenly the window just ahead was flung wide open. The shutter banged on the wall right beside him. If he'd been one pace on, he'd have been knocked out cold on the pavement.

He halted. Even with the relaxed rules in carnival season, the club ought to be closed at this hour. He glanced into the open window, expecting to see a few intoxicated patrons still partying, but no noise streamed out. No endless thud, thud, thud of drum and bass. No high-pitched giggles, loud laughs or low murmurs. It seemed there was no one in the vast room—until something white silently flashed in the deep recesses. He looked closer, tracking the fast-moving creature as the white flashed again. The woman wore a loose white top and…nothing else? The most basic instinct had him locking on her legs—unbelievably long legs that right now were moving unbelievably fast.

Pyjamas. *Short* pyjamas.

His suddenly slushy brain slowly reached a conclusion. She opened another window down the side of the room and turned again. She wore ballet flats on her feet, not for fashion, but for function, dancing across the floor—spinning so quickly her auburn hair swirled in a curling ribbon behind her. She leapt and landed near the window on the opposite side of the room and opened that one with another dramatic, effervescent gesture before turning yet again. That was when he saw her face properly for the first time.

She was smiling. Not one of the usual sorts

of smiles Antonio received—not awed or nervous or curious or come-hitherish… This smile was so full of raw joy it made him feel he should step back into the darkness, but he couldn't find the will to turn away.

Heat kicked hard in his gut.

Anger. Not lust. *Never* lust.

He'd have to have spent the last six months living under a rock not to know she'd moved to San Felipe. Given he ruled the island principality, he knew exactly who she was and why she was here. And he didn't give a damn that she was even more stunning in real life than in any of the pictures saturating the Internet. Bella Sanchez was here to cause trouble. And Antonio didn't want trouble in San Felipe.

Nor did he want Bella Sanchez.

He didn't want anyone.

Yet here he was with his feet glued to the pavement, watching her whirl her way round the room with glorious abandon, from one window to the next in flying leaps until she'd opened them all.

She executed another series of dizzying spins across the floor, and suddenly stopped—positioned smack bang in the centre of the window frame he was looking through.

'Enjoying the view?' Her smile had vanished and her voice dripped with sarcasm.

When he didn't move, she glided closer, her feline green eyes like lasers. She wasn't even breathless as she stared him down like a Fury about to wreak revenge on a miscreant.

Antonio's reflexes snapped. She thought she could shame him into scuttling away? Another hit of heat made him clench his muscles. He pushed back the hood of his sweatshirt and coolly gazed back up at her, grimly anticipating her recognition of him.

Her eyes widened instantly but she quickly schooled the shock from her face—her expression smoothing until she became inscrutable. Somehow she stood taller. She had the straightest back of anyone he'd ever seen.

'Your Highness,' she said crisply. 'May I help you with something?'

Unfortunately he couldn't reply; his tongue was cleaved to the roof of his mouth. How could she look this radiant so early in the morning? She had to have had an extremely late night and yet here she was without a scrap of make-up on, looking intolerably beautiful.

Antonio actively avoided being alone with women—especially models, actresses and socialites—but, given his single status and

Crown Prince title, they littered his path and made their play nonetheless. Over the past few years he'd met hundreds, if not thousands, of stunning, willing women. He'd refused every single one.

But none had ever looked as gorgeous as Bella Sanchez did right now. And none had looked as haughty.

At his continued silence, she stepped closer. 'You were spying on me?'

His anger sharpened. He'd avoided meeting *her* most of all and now she made him sound like a peeping Tom. No matter that in part he felt like one.

'It is past closing hours,' he said stiffly.

'You're policing me?' As she stared down at him that haughty barrier locked fully into place, leaching the last of the vitality in her eyes. 'The club is closed.'

Her English accent was muddied. He figured it was from the years she'd spent abroad and the mix of people in her life.

'I'm merely ventilating the rooms,' she explained.

'Getting rid of suspicious smells?' He'd heard the rumours and he wasn't going to ignore them.

A small smile emerged, nothing like the earlier one. 'This is a non-smoking venue, not some den of iniquity.'

'There are other vices,' he replied with calm consideration. 'Salvatore Accardi warned me this operation was going to bring San Felipe nothing but trouble.'

'He would know all about trouble.'

She didn't so much as blink as she snapped back her answer.

He'd wanted to see her reaction to his reference to Accardi—but he'd got almost none.

Salvatore Accardi, former Italian politician, had taken up permanent residence in his San Felipe holiday home. And Salvatore Accardi was reputedly Bella Sanchez's father.

Twenty-odd years ago she'd been born of scandal, supposedly the love child of the married Salvatore and his sex-symbol mistress. Their affair had been splashed across all the newspapers of the day. But Salvatore had never acknowledged Bella as his baby. He'd refused to undergo paternity testing. He'd stayed with his long-suffering wife, pregnant at the time, and raised their daughter, who'd been born a mere three months before Bella.

Bella had been raised in the public eye, eventually dancing professionally before becoming chatelaine of this party house in the heart of Antonio's principality. And according to Salvatore Accardi now, her presence would attract nothing but sleaze to San Felipe.

'Is it so terrible to provide a place for people to have fun?' Bella asked, shrugging one of her delicate shoulders. She looked slender, but strong.

Antonio frowned at the direction—distraction—of his thoughts.

'This isn't about that,' he said coldly. 'This is revenge. This is setting up so you're right in Accardi's face.'

'Is that what he told you?' Her poise cracked briefly as anger flashed. 'Do you honestly think you can believe everything—or *anything*—he says?'

At a gut level Antonio had never much liked Salvatore Accardi, but nothing had ever been proven. All those rumours of corporate and political corruption had remained only rumours. And if the man had the personal morals of an alley cat, that was his own business. He'd owned property in San Felipe for too long for Antonio to find reason to require him to leave.

Just as there'd been no reason to refuse a work permit and residency to Bella Sanchez.

And didn't everyone have the right to be believed innocent until proven guilty?

In her white short pyjamas Bella looked both innocent and unbearably sensual, because that white cotton was thin and she wore nothing beneath it. And when she moved? He could see the outline of her slim waist and generous curves.

'I'm not sure a venue like this suits San Felipe,' he said tightly.

'As if there aren't other clubs?' she questioned softly but her gaze was sharp. She almost leaned out of the window frame, making him acutely aware of her unfettered breasts. 'This isn't a sex club. There are no pole dancers or strippers.' She lingered over her quiet words, but then her eyes glinted. 'Definitely no drugs in dodgy back-room deals.'

Her voice shook with fierceness. He knew her mother, Madeline Sanchez, one of the world's greatest 'mistresses' in a time when such things had been scandalous, had overdosed more than a year ago in a Parisian apartment. Everybody knew all there was to know about Bella Sanchez.

'This is a legitimate bar and dance floor,' she added more calmly. 'And I'm a responsible club owner.'

'You're young and inexperienced.' He paused

pointedly. 'In managing a commercial enterprise, that is.'

Her eyes widened, for a split second she looked furious. But he watched the change as she controlled her emotions once more—the stiffening of that already ramrod-straight spine, her smile so different from the one earlier, the hint of calculation as she glanced at his casual attire.

He braced. She was sizing him up and about to fire her own shot. And oddly, he was looking forward to it.

She swept her arm across her body in a dramatic gesture, drawing his attention to her attributes once more. 'Why don't you come in and find out for yourself?' she invited in a sultry tone. 'Come inside and see if you can find anything wrong with my club.'

It was a blatant dare—she'd switched into 'Bella Sanchez, Sex Symbol' without skipping a beat.

But it wasn't *that* challenge that did it for him. Not that coy smile of sophisticated amusement. It was the emotion lurking in the backs of her eyes. The anger she was trying hard to control—that slight tremor in her fingers before she curled them into a fist.

'Yes.'

He said it because she didn't expect him to. She thought he'd politely and coldly refuse, smile distantly and retreat, like the conservative Crown Prince he was. She'd called his bluff.

So he'd called hers. Because at this moment, he damn well felt like doing the last thing anyone—least of all her—expected.

And she hadn't expected it. Her shock flashed for one satisfying second.

He waited while she unbolted the heavy door, opened it and stepped aside for him to enter. He paused just inside the room, watching as she closed the door and marched around him to lead the way.

'No suspicious smells, see,' she said pointedly. 'Nothing illegal.'

The ground-floor space was sleek and smelled clean, not yet permeated with the lingering, less than fragrant scent of five hundred sweaty clubbers dancing there night after night.

He glanced up—away from the back view of her never-ending legs—and saw the decadent wallpaper and the wrought-iron railings protecting patrons who wanted to party on the mezzanine floor. The chandeliers gleamed even this early in the morning. He hadn't been in a nightclub in a decade. He'd been crowned in his early twenties, but had been aware of the restraints on his behaviour for years before that. He'd always been dutiful. He'd had to be.

Only now he felt the stirrings of a desire he'd buried deep all those years ago. When *had* he last danced?

'You'll want to see the liquor licence.' She stalked over to the main bar. 'And there it is, exactly where it should be. The emergency exits are well marked,' she added, all officiousness. 'It was formerly a fire station, you know.'

He did know. But there'd be no putting out the fire in her eyes.

'The rest of the paperwork is upstairs,' she said defiantly, turning to face him.

'So lead the way,' he answered bluntly. He was committed now.

For a split second her shock was visible again.

Yes, Crown Prince Antonio would never ordinarily go up into the back room of a notorious nightclub in the sole company of a supposedly scandalous siren…but he felt like doing it just to see that reaction again.

He suppressed a smile as he followed her to one of the winding staircases that were like pillars at each side of the room. But as he climbed behind her his amusement faded.

He hadn't been so alone with a woman so barely attired in years. And it shouldn't have been a problem now. Except her legs went on for ever. He tried to tear his attention from them. Failed. Was relieved when they reached the mezzanine and she darted ahead to open another window. She then headed to a small alcove that hid a door marked 'Private'.

Another flight of stairs.

This time he gave in to the temptation to look. She would never know. But there was the faintest flush on her porcelain cheeks as she waited for him to walk into her office.

The top floor was clearly her private space and very different from the dark and sensual decor of the club downstairs. This room was lighter, with white walls and a cream rug covering the floorboards. A large desk dominated the room. A laptop sat open on it, paper files spread beside it. A filing cabinet was behind the desk, while a couple of chairs sat at angles in front of it. But Antonio remained standing because there was another door—open—through which he could see a small kitchenette. And given she was wearing pyjamas, he figured it was safe to assume there was a bed in there too. Tension hit. This had been a mistake. And Antonio couldn't afford any mistakes.

Bella stared. Crown Prince Antonio De Santis had accepted her challenge and was standing in her small office. She'd thought he'd decline, all unbending regal politeness. But it seemed he really had chosen this morning to inspect her business—obscenely early, name-dropping the man who refused to acknowledge her and dressed like *that*.

She'd recognised him the second he'd pulled back the hood of his sweatshirt but he looked nothing like the austere Crown Prince she'd seen on screens and in magazines. That man was tall and broad-shouldered, with not a hair out of place and almost always dressed in an immaculate midnight-blue suit. Perfect for the reserved, always polite but distant Prince.

The man in front of her now hadn't shaved. His hair was mussed. He must have been out running or something what with the old sweatshirt, track pants and trainers he was wearing. And the edge she'd glimpsed in his eyes? She never would have expected that. Nor would she have expected to feel breathless and hot in his company. Not so hyper-aware.

She never felt that around any guy.

'You'll find everything is in there.' She opened the file and turned it so he could read it, reading it upside down herself. She wanted him to see every single piece of paper and be satisfied and leave as soon as possible. She wasn't going down without a fight. She'd prove to all her doubters that she could manage this club. She'd prove it to *him*.

So never mind that she was in her shortie pyjamas, her top slightly too loose and with no bra beneath, because she couldn't be embarrassed. Never mind that she'd only managed two hours' sleep because she had so much to do. The club had been open only a week and, while it looked promising, she had a long, long way to go before it could be declared a success and she could sell up and start up the business of her heart.

But he didn't say anything about the paperwork. She glanced up and caught him staring at her. Again.

She was used to men looking. They all wanted the same thing, right? They all thought they knew everything there was to know about her. But the ice in this man's eyes was something else. It burned.

He stood silent. Guarded. *Judging.*

She'd not expected that from San Felipe's

broken, beloved Prince. Wasn't he supposed to hide a wounded heart? Wasn't he supposed to be kind and benevolent under the weight of all that duty?

Everyone knew his story. His 'One True Love' had tragically died of cancer barely two months after his coronation and the accident that had claimed the lives of both his parents. He'd not been linked to another woman since. The Prince had buried his heart with his girlfriend. And, according to the glossy mags, the nation believed only the love of a pure and perfect woman could heal him and bring him happiness…

That woman clearly wasn't her given he was looking at her like *that*.

Forbidding. Disapproving.

Thrown off balance, she felt goaded into provoking a reaction from him. Beneath the fifty feet of ice he hid behind, it had to be there—emotion of *some* kind.

She should have been intimidated. She should have remained polite. She should have respected the power he held. But she was too tired. And too hurt.

'Why are you staring at me like I've forgotten something?' She stepped out from her desk. 'Should I have curtseyed as you walked in?' She lifted her chin at his utter impassivity. 'Should I get on my knees before you?'

She regretted the sultry taunt the second she'd uttered it.

Because there was no reaction. He didn't move a muscle. Didn't speak a word. Just kept, ever so coolly, regarding her.

Her cheeks burned as shame grew. She'd been everything the world expected her to be—a scandalous, tarty temptress. But she was a big fat faker.

And he wasn't. He really was as frozen-hearted as they said. And every bit as breath-taking.

'You're going to have to do better than that,' he finally said. 'Do you think you're the first woman to try seducing me by stripping and dancing in front of me?'

His words hit like hailstones.

'I didn't strip.'

'Only because you didn't bother getting dressed properly.'

'And I didn't dance for you.' She ignored his interruption. 'I was just warming up alone. You're the one who stopped to watch. You could have kept walking, Tony.'

For a split second she got a reaction—his

jaw dropped. Before he snapped it shut and then shot his words like bullets.

'What did you just call me?'

'Tony,' she repeated, refusing to back down. 'Crown Prince Antonio is too much of a mouthful.'

There was a pause, then his gaze skittered down her body—so deliberately. 'Too much of a mouthful,' he echoed slowly.

This time *Bella's* jaw dropped. Did he say that while scoping out her breasts? Which, yes, were on the fuller side. Especially for a dancer.

Crossing his arms, he continued to regard her, making her feel uncharacteristically vulnerable. His complete attention wasn't like any ordinary audience of thousands. His scrutiny was way more intense.

'I've seen it all, every artifice, every attempt to attract me,' he muttered. 'It won't work.'

'Because we're all out to entrap you?' she asked, shocked at his direct approach. 'You think I'm trying to use my feminine wiles to draw you in? Because you're the biggest prize?'

'Aren't you?' he answered, cocking his head. 'Or are you just trying to provoke me? You want to win a reaction from "the Ice Prince",' he mocked. 'Because you're all about getting the reaction.'

She drew breath at the accuracy of his hit.

'I've had every kind of play,' he continued with a quietness that belied the edge to his words. 'The sympathy, simpering agreement and the bitchy comebacks of the treat-me-mean kind…there's nothing I haven't seen or heard, so don't bother.'

Anger rushed along her veins, scalding her skin. 'You think I want you anywhere near me?'

His lips twisted in a coolly mocking look and he didn't bother to answer.

'You're unbelievably arrogant,' she said.

'You think?'

Yes, she did. But swirling beneath the frost-covered atmosphere was elemental attraction at its most basic. He was appallingly attractive—her body yearned to get closer to his. And when he didn't back away from her challenge?

Primitive instinct could be a powerful thing. But she had more of a brain than that. So her basic instinct could go bury itself back in the cave it had been dwelling in for the last three years.

'I have no desire to attract you,' she declared passionately. Totally meaning every word. 'This isn't some *ploy* with which I hope to gain your grace or favour or sexual interest. You do not interest me in the least.'

'You interest me,' he said softly, slicing the ground from under her.

Sensual awareness feathered over her skin.

'Why San Felipe?' He stepped closer. 'Why now?'

Her heart stopped beating as she looked up into his blue eyes. For a second he actually looked human—as if he actually cared. And for a second she longed to open up and just be honest.

But as if she could ever tell him. When he'd so arrogantly assumed she wanted to land herself a princely lover? When he chose to listen to the father who'd always refused to recognise her?

He'd be just another man who denied her.

She wanted him to leave but she couldn't tear her gaze from his. She'd thought she could handle anything. But she wasn't sure she could handle him.

He reached out as if to take her hand. 'Why now, Bella?'

Abruptly she turned to avoid his touch.

'Careful—'

His warning came too late. As she whirled to escape her weak ankle went and she stumbled, catching her thigh on the corner of her desk.

Antonio winced at the grimace of pain on Bella's face as she grabbed the desk to stop herself falling down. She'd gashed her leg, just above her knee. As he looked close he saw a long, jagged scar running in a wonky line up her shin.

She paled, her lips pressed together to mute any sound of pain.

It had been so long since he'd had any kind of physical comfort. Or offered any. He'd almost forgotten how. 'Bella?'

'It's fine.' She straightened and drew in a deep breath.

'I'm sure,' he replied, but he knew it wasn't.

'Wouldn't want you thinking this was another ploy.'

'It is my fault you fell,' he said stiffly, his hands at his side, wanting to help her yet feeling oddly impotent.

'You feel responsible? Rest easy, I won't sue you.' Her lips compressed. 'It's no more damaged than it already was.'

'It still needs dressing.' Blood was already

oozing from the small wound. 'You have a first-aid kit?'

'Of course.' She didn't move.

He sighed at her reluctance. 'I need to see it. Or I'll revoke your operating licence.'

She gritted her teeth and limped behind her desk. His irritation smouldered. She really didn't want him to help. Was that because he'd really offended her or because he'd struck too close to the mark?

She *had* been trying to get a rise out of him, but she hadn't meant the vampish 'on her knees' offer—not when she'd jumped to get away from him.

She clutched the small container but he held out his hand. Sending him a death look, she passed it to him. Antonio bit back the smile of satisfaction and opened the lid.

'Lean on the desk,' he told her.

'This isn't necessary.'

He wasn't used to repeating instructions. He glanced up and her stormy expression clashed with his. 'Lean on the desk.'

Slowly, stiffly, she rested her body back.

'Thank you,' he said, ultra-politely.

He knelt at her feet, inwardly grimacing at the irony given her provocative remark only moments ago.

He knew an injury had ended her professional career. In the last decade Antonio had attended the ballet only out of duty but he could appreciate the strength and commitment it would have taken Bella to reach the level she had.

Her body was still incredibly athletic. This close he could smell her light, floral scent. It made him think of summer sun, not endless nights in a darkened dance club. In his mind's eye he saw her on the floor, bumping and grinding up close to her patrons. He gritted his teeth. Not jealous. And *not* aroused.

He was *not* aroused by her.

He wasn't like all the other red-blooded men in the world. He didn't have time to be. He didn't have the right. But just at this moment, he was every *inch* a mere man.

'Do you dance your way through all your tasks?' he asked, trying to distract himself from her sweet scent and delicate skin. He dabbed the blood and prepped a plaster as quickly as he could, not touching any part of her beyond necessary.

'Is that a serious question?' she mumbled.

'Yes.' Satisfied with how the plaster neatly covered the gash, he glanced up to read her expression. She was sitting unnaturally still—apparently holding her breath.

She met his gaze with those deep green eyes that were now almost liquid. 'You want to know if I dance while brushing my teeth?'

He inwardly smiled at the image. 'I bet you brush in time to the music playing in your head.'

Her eyes widened and *her* smile broke free—her full mouth softened and her eyes sparkled. She looked fresh and beautiful and bright.

Heat flared from flicker to flame, urging him to touch those lush curving lips—

He jerked to his feet and stepped away before he did something colossally stupid.

'Have you been out drinking?'

He turned at the bitterness in her tone and saw her smile had vanished.

'I don't drink,' he said simply.

'No vices at all?' she mocked. 'No sex, right?'

That speculation was correct. It had been years since he'd had a lover. He was only about duty: to serve his country and to protect his people. *All* of them—dead and alive. That was his penance.

'And no drinking,' she added. 'I guess that just leaves drugs.'

'None of those either.'

'Fast cars?'

He shook his head. 'The Crown Prince cannot be injured or killed in a car accident. That can't happen in San Felipe again.' His parents' tragedy had cut the nation too deeply.

'So you're reduced to *watching*.' Storms gathered in her eyes.

'If you wanted privacy you would have kept your curtains closed,' he answered abruptly. 'But you didn't, because you like to be watched. You've made a career out of it.'

Anger flashed in her face. Before she could reply a short melody burst through the charged atmosphere. Then again. And again. His damn cell phone.

'Are you going to answer that or would you like me to?' Those temptress tones returned—but so shaky this time.

She was trying to goad him again, using her voice, her eyes, her femininity to bring a man to his knees.

Not this man. He wasn't that weak.

Yet she knew that already. And that was the twist. She expected him to pull away—she wanted to drive him further back because she didn't want him too close. Because *his* nearness bothered *her*.

That realisation shocked him. His body had already betrayed him. She was so damn beautiful, for the first time in years his desire was stirred.

'It's my security team.' He cleared the frog from his throat and ignored the call.

'I'm amazed they let you wander the streets alone,' she said dryly.

'They know exactly where I am.'

Her eyebrows lifted. 'You told them you were coming here?'

'GPS.' His watch was tracked. It even had a silent emergency alarm button. Very spy film but he'd had to agree to it to get his morning walks alone.

'Your every movement is accounted for? So you're like a prisoner on electronic monitoring?'

'The concept is not dissimilar. They're concerned because I've not returned to the palace by my usual time.' He pulled the phone from his pocket as it began to ring again. If he didn't reply to this next call, a security team would be on its way in seconds.

'A change in the usual routine,' she drawled. 'Heaven forbid.'

'Yet here you are, doing the same warm-up dance routine you've been doing for years,' he answered blandly. 'We are creatures of habit, just doing what we usually do.'

Like falling back on old defences.

But as he read the message from his security chief he tensed. He double-checked the time on the screen—how had twenty minutes passed so quickly? He crossed the room to glance out of the window. In the space of a few minutes, the world had changed.

Outside people were lining the barricaded street, already standing two to three deep. He'd been so engrossed in dealing with Bella he hadn't heard the crowds gathering.

Swiftly he stepped back. To be seen inside Bella Sanchez's apartment at this hour of the morning would be unacceptable. But to be seen leaving it even worse. Especially given his unshaven, dishevelled appearance. The world would think he'd had another kind of workout altogether.

His gut burned.

Was this *want*? It had been so damn long since he'd wanted any woman. Clenching the phone in his fist, he faced her. She'd stilled, listening to the rising clamour outside. Given the way her features had tightened, the realisation the world had woken wasn't good news for her either.

'It seems it is your lucky day,' he muttered, feeling like provoking her the way she had him. 'I will have to remain here.'

Her eyes widened. 'For how long?'

Until his team could work out a subtle extraction plan. 'Until they've all gone home.'

'But that race won't finish for another six hours!'

Her obvious discomfort gave him a macabre pleasure. That she didn't want him near echoed his own unwanted feelings.

But he looked at her, outwardly unmoved. 'What do you suggest we do to pass the time?'

CHAPTER TWO

BELLA STARED. HE was joking, wasn't he? But Prince Antonio never joked; he looked as straight up serious and remote as ever. Worse, if anything.

'Why can't you leave now?' She still didn't understand why he was here at all.

He stepped further from the window, looking at his phone as it buzzed again. 'The crowds outside are already too big.'

'They love their Crown Prince. They'll be happy to see you.' He could do no wrong in his people's eyes.

'I'm not prepared for a meet and greet at this point in time.' He quickly sent a text.

'Because you're not in one of your navy suits? The track pants aren't all bad…' In the baggy hoodie he looked younger and more approachable than in any of the stills she'd seen. In fact dressed like this he looked alarmingly attractive. 'A prince at leisure—'

He glanced up and her words died in her throat. It finally dawned on her why he refused to leave.

'You don't want them to see you here,' she said. 'With me.'

He didn't answer. Didn't need to. She could see it all over his icy expression.

He was loath to be seen anywhere near her. Why? Did he think she could taint him in some way?

That hurt where she was most vulnerable. No one—not her old dance company, not her ex-boyfriend, not even her own *father*—wanted to claim a personal connection to her. Only those wanting instant Internet fame wanted to be caught near her. And as if that were what he wanted. Like her, Crown Prince Antonio De Santis had been born famous, but he was legitimately so—whereas she?

He steadily held her gaze. That unnerving reserve made her too aware of him, but she refused to let him silence her with little more than a stare. Not now or ever.

'You think it would damage your reputation to be seen exiting my club at this hour of the morning?' Her voice shook and she drew in a sharp breath. 'Maybe it would *enhance* it.'

He still didn't answer but his demeanour

changed. He might be wearing worn workout gear, but now he looked every inch the powerful 'Head of State'. Clothes made no difference. Nothing could pierce that princely aura. Bella's anger flared. He was so protected, whereas she?

'No one would believe anything "untoward" of you. But me?' She laughed bitterly. 'I'm the vixen, right? But surely not even wicked little Bella Sanchez could trap Prince Antonio with her wiles…'

It was what he'd accused her of attempting only moments before. And he was right, it was laughable. Scathing, she stepped closer; her words tumbled unchecked, unthinking.

'I don't know why you're so worried,' she snarled. 'You're untemptable, right? You're the frigid Prince.' She took no notice of his sudden frown or the muscle jerking in his jaw; his wordless judgment had unleashed the banked-up bitterness of so many betrayals. 'Your absolute rejection of any physical intimacy is cowardly.'

Just as hiding here for hours would be cowardly.

And dangerous for her.

'In what way?' he asked icily, his words

sharply enunciated. 'Doesn't it denote self-control?'

Something burned in his eyes now, but she was too hurt to take heed and too hurt to stop herself lashing out. 'Maybe you're afraid that once you start, you won't be able to stop.'

He said nothing. He didn't need to. His rigidity screamed irritation and arrogance.

'Everyone loses control some time,' she taunted. She'd seen it every night since she'd opened the club. People got carried away. Just as she was now. But she didn't care.

'Not me,' he finally countered.

'Because you're a robot?' she scoffed. 'You're just a prince—that doesn't give you super powers.'

Silence strained for two beats before he broke it with a soft-spoken, hard-hitting whisper. 'You want me to prove it?'

He didn't move a muscle, but somehow he made the room smaller. The subtlest change in his tone, the darkening in his eyes put her senses on alert. He'd gone from angered, to something else altogether. Something more dangerous.

Goosebumps rose on her skin, but deep down satisfaction flickered. 'You don't have to prove anything to me.'

'Don't I? When you've taken it upon yourself to judge me so completely?'

'You'd judged me before you even crossed my threshold,' she pointed out with relish. 'And you collude with other people's judgments when you react with concern about being seen in my company.'

'You're mistaken in many ways.' He frowned. 'I'm not a robot. And no, I don't have super powers. But I don't lose control, Bella.'

He walked closer, until he loomed in front of her. She held her ground and watched. *Dared.*

'I can start,' he promised with wintry imperiousness. 'And then stop.'

'Start what?' she taunted again.

'You're Bella Sanchez,' he murmured. 'You live for kisses and adoration.'

That stung. Her mother's reputation had stained her own from the start. Men assumed that as she'd inherited her mother's figure, she'd have her 'skills' too. But her mother had been discarded by every one of her many lovers. Which was partly why Bella was *not* the lover of anyone bold enough to make a move. And the truth was she was unmoved. Always.

She should shake him off with some glib retort and a smile and make her escape from a situation like this the way she'd done many times before. Or she should tell him exactly where to go and why.

'What if I don't want you to kiss me?' she asked, determinedly standing in place despite the adrenalin rush urging her to run.

'Don't you?' He laughed then. A low, sexy, mocking laugh.

That he'd laughed at all was a shock, but that he laughed like that? She just gazed at him, stunned by this glimpse of someone else altogether—a gorgeous virile man.

His smile disappeared as he neared, but there was still that glimpse of human behind the pale blue. 'You are beautiful.'

Beneath that clinical assessment she heard huskiness. Heat washed over her, confusing her more.

'Beauty isn't everything,' she pointed out.

Glossy magazines and plastic surgeons would argue otherwise, but Bella knew the truth. Beauty faded. Beauty depended on who was looking. Beauty didn't count for anything at the end of the day.

'No,' he agreed softly.

The atmosphere thickened, building the tension both within her and between them. She wanted to duck and run. She already knew she wouldn't feel anything if he kissed her. She never felt anything. That was the point. She'd tried but she wasn't the hedonist the world wanted her to be. In ten seconds it would be obvious who the frigid one was. He'd know her secret. She gritted her teeth, angered by that old humiliation.

'Go on, then,' she finally snapped. 'Try it and see what happens.'

'Such an invitation,' he mocked.

'You're hardly bounding over with unbridled lust.'

'I don't do unbridled lust, remember?' He regarded her intently. 'You're not going to drive me crazy.'

It was almost as if he was challenging himself. Not her.

'I don't want to drive anyone crazy,' she retorted. 'People ought to take responsibility for their own actions.'

She just wanted to do her own thing. She hadn't asked to be raised in the glare of paparazzi flashes. Yes, she'd chosen the ballet stage, but it wasn't supposed to have intruded into her personal life as much. And now she did all that Internet sharing only to build something for the future—funding her escape route.

'Indeed they should.' He gripped her waist, his hands not too high or too low or too tight.

He didn't step closer so there was a clear two inches between them. He held her in the position perfect for a formal dance. But they weren't in a ballroom. They were yards from her tiny bedroom.

Heart thudding, Bella fisted her hands and held them to her stomach, but she couldn't bring herself to say *stop.* Instinctively she knew that if she did, he would. But she was curious to see how far perfect Prince Antonio would take this. She kept her eyes open, focusing intently on him. It was a trick she'd learned when amorous dates had moved closer than she'd wanted. Guys didn't like to think they weren't wowing a woman with their sensual prowess.

But Antonio kept his eyes open too. As he inclined his head she found herself sinking into their surprising depths—they were such a pale blue, but there was an echo of that smile glinting in the backs of them. That smile was what she really wanted more of.

He pressed his lips to hers in the lightest caress, offering less than a heartbeat of touch. But it delivered a lightning flash of heat. Bella froze, teetering on the edge of something unknown, so tempted to tumble over—but he didn't take her there. He didn't touch her again.

He remained a breath away but she couldn't fathom his feelings in his unreadable eyes.

Finally it dawned on her that he had no feelings. He'd been teasing her. He'd intended to give her nothing but that chaste peck all along. Perfectly, bloodlessly executed. Any second now he'd step back and say, 'I told you so'. He was utterly in control at all times.

Disappointment spilled into that vast, empty space in her chest. She really shouldn't feel it, she really shouldn't care, she should concede his victory with laughing grace and push him away.

But she'd felt a glimmer of what might have been—a sliver of heat that had stunned her with its strength.

So she could only stay still, unable to move for thinking—for *feeling*. His eyes were so damn mesmerising but now she couldn't bear to look into them any more. Yet when she dropped her gaze, she saw his sensual mouth and his chiselled jaw roughened with morning stubble. He was picture-postcard perfect and it was so unfair because for one millisecond she'd actually *wanted*—

His fingers tightened, pinching her waist. She looked up in surprise but before she could speak his lips brushed hers again. Another soft, too brief—tantalising—caress. She got the smallest glimpse into his eyes before he bent to her again. His reserve crumbled as intensity flared. Her heart stopped at that flash of emotion.

When he kissed her that third time, he lingered. She lifted her chin, meeting him, her body instinctively yearning for him to stay. She wanted more—a *real* kiss. She wanted him to release the energy she sensed building within him and ease the need starting to ache within her. She wanted more of the magic she'd tasted in that first swift touch. She wanted more than disillusionment and emptiness and abandonment all over again. She just wanted *more*.

For the first time in her life, she *really* wanted it.

He didn't disappoint her this time. He stayed. He held. He kissed. His lips moved from gentle, to more insistent, to finally demanding. As she acquiesced, parting her mouth, his demands grew greater still. His hands shifted, shaping her curves and then possessively pulling her closer. Her heart struck up again, sprinting to a frantic tempo—in shock. In passion. She wriggled her hands from where they'd been squashed between them and reached up to his shoulders so she could literally hang on as he bent her backwards and kissed her more thoroughly still.

Oh, he kissed her. Her eyes drifted shut as she focused on the pressure of his lips—the teasing pleasure. His kiss lightened and she gripped his shoulders more tightly, afraid he was about to pull away. But he kissed her again and again in a series that mimicked that first—softly stirring desire, building her frustration until she couldn't control the small moan that escaped. Then he kissed her hard and long again. And he repeated the pattern—unpredictable, maddening. Delicious.

She'd never have expected Prince Antonio to be as playful. Or as skilled. But what did it matter when he made her feel like *this*?

She moaned in pleasure as he kissed her deeply again. It was as if all the empty places within her were being filled and heated and the sensation was so addictive. There was pure pleasure to be had in his arms. The kind she'd never experienced with anyone else.

Breathless, she wanted to say something, but couldn't. She didn't want to break the magic—uncaring of any consequences, of how crazy this had suddenly become. She just wanted to feel it—all of him—all of the gratification she could get. Instinctively she moved, circling her hips. His hand slid, pressing over the curve of her bottom and pulling her harder against the heat of his pelvis. Feeling how aroused he was made her melt all the more into his embrace.

His arms tightened around her but she didn't resist as he walked her backwards and then pushed her back against the desk. She couldn't remain standing anyway and she had no desire to stop. She only wanted more. Just here. Now. In this white-hot moment.

He shoved the files behind her to the floor with a sweep of his arm, pushed her back until she lay on the hard wood, and followed her down.

He kissed down the side of her neck, burying his mouth in that sensitive spot where her neck met her shoulders. His hand slid beneath her light pyjama top. The sensation of skin on skin made her arch involuntarily. His hand was heavy, then light, teasing as he traced small circles over her abdomen, up to her ribs, then higher still. She shivered as he neared the hard peak of her breast. He lifted his head from hers, breaking the kiss to look into her eyes. He didn't look down as he lifted her top to expose her breasts. She felt the cool air, felt her nipples tighten more—until they were almost painful. She licked her dried lips as she waited, splayed on the desk beneath him, until he looked down at her partially naked body.

A groan ripped from him when he finally looked. She looked down too, saw how her breasts thrust up towards him, her nipples tight and needy and erect—begging for more than his visual attention. They wanted touch. He muttered something unintelligible. Before she could ask him what he'd said he bent his head and took her nipple in the hot cavern of his mouth. Her breathing came quick and erratic as she watched him take pleasure in her body—in pleasuring *her.*

She closed her eyes, sprawled back on the desk, basking in the sensations as he explored her more fully. He pushed between her legs, grinding against her, and cupped her other breast in his hand, his fingers teasing that taut peak. When he pushed her full breasts together to lave both nipples with his tongue, she almost arched off the wood completely. All her restraints were now off, her need unleashed. She bucked, thrusting her hips against his, wanting him to strip her, touch her and kiss her where she was hot and wet and so, so ready.

Never had she been ready for a man the way she was for him. Never had a man made her feel this aroused. The ache between her legs burned, her blood ran faster in a quickening beat of need. She reached out, wanting to explore him too. His skin was hot to the touch. His jaw bristled but it was so good as it gently abraded her tender skin. She raked her hands across his back, the heat of him burning through his sweatshirt.

His muscularity surprised her. He was only ever pictured in suits so she'd never have guessed he'd be this defined. Granite muscles like these meant he worked out—regularly and hard. She wanted to see them. Wanted to touch. But he pressed down, smothering her attempts to pull his sweatshirt up, distracting her from that goal by simply kissing her again and again and again while running his hands over her bared breasts with wicked skill.

And she couldn't resist succumbing to the pleasure of it.

That it could be this man who pulled this feeling from her? This unadulterated *lust*. He left no room for regret or reason. There was only this, only now. His breathing roughened but he said nothing more. He kissed down her neck, then lower to tease with fiery touches across her quivering belly, then back up to her breasts. But his hand worked lower, slipping beneath the waistband of her flimsy short pyjama bottoms. She parted her legs further without thinking about it, aching for him to touch her there. He growled guttural approval as his fingers cupped her intimately. She shuddered at the intensity of desire that consumed her as he gently stroked. She was so close. The pleasure built so shockingly quickly. She'd never been so close with anyone.

'Antonio…' She breathed the quietest plea as she arched against him, right on the edge.

He froze, then glanced up to look into her eyes for a heartbeat. Dazed, she didn't register his tormented expression. But then he pulled away from her, his face now utterly impassive.

'You're stopping?' She gasped in disbelief. *'Now?'*

His lips twisted but he didn't reply. Running his hand through his hair, he huffed out a harsh breath and stepped back from her.

Astonished, she stared, realising what he'd done. He'd done this to prove a petty point. And he'd proved it already. But it was also a punishment. He was putting her in her place in a humiliating show of power—he could have her any way he wanted, however he chose.

But now he chose not to.

That he'd use his sensual dominance over her this way was most especially cruel because she'd never felt anything like this. No man had made her *want* in this way and this one time she'd almost felt pure, sensual pleasure, it had been snatched from her. She swept her hand over her belly, as if she could press away the ache deep inside.

'I don't need you,' she muttered angrily. So hurt. 'I don't need *any* man.' She didn't need any *one*.

He turned back, his gaze smouldering. Her legs were still splayed. She was so exposed, half-stripped and spread on her own damn desk for him to toy with but she refused to cover up and show how shamed she felt.

'What are you doing?' His words sounded raw and accusing.

She realised he was staring at her hand pressed low on her belly. Bitterness rose in her throat. Because yes, the only way she'd ever experienced an orgasm was by her own action. But as if she'd do that now?

Heat burned in his narrowed eyes. Outrage burned in her. She wasn't giving him the pleasure of *watching*. She curled her fingers into a fist, her vision swimming with acidic tears.

She heard his groan and a muttered word, but she didn't know what he said because suddenly he was there. Back where she needed him. Bending between her parted thighs, his spread hand raking up her body.

'It wouldn't be as good,' he muttered, leaning close, catching her gaze with his.

She tried to turn her head away but he moved too fast, holding her chin with a firm grip. He almost smiled as he moved closer.

This kiss was cautious and tender.

She didn't close her eyes and when he drew back a fraction to gauge her response, she kept glaring at him. But then he kissed one eyelid. Then the other. Making her close her eyes. Then he caught her mouth with his again. Not cautious at all. Not holding anything back. Just that passionate teasing, stirring her to react again. To want.

And heaven help her she did. So quickly she was there again, lost in the lust he roused within her. She couldn't wriggle away from him. Couldn't break the kiss. Rather she moaned in his mouth—a mixture of hurt and want and pleading.

In answer he slid his hand firmly over her stomach, wrapped his broad palm around her fist and lifted her arm, pressing it back on the desk beside her, clearing his path down her body. He cupped her breast, then teased his way lower again, to where she was still wet and hot and wanting. All the while his lips were sealed to hers, his tongue stroking and teasing and claiming her the way the rest of her wanted to be claimed.

She moaned again, nothing but want this time. She wanted him naked, wanted to touch him everywhere, wanted him to thrust deep inside her and ease this hellish ache. He didn't. He just teased—decadently, mercilessly until she was sweat-slicked and shivering and mindless.

She bucked against his hand—wanting faster, deeper, more. He groaned in approval, kissing her harder, letting her feel more of his weight. She wanted to take it all. Her hips rocked, undulating in an increasing rhythm, matching the stroke of his fingers and tongue. She wanted to force him to break free of his control. She wanted him to stop holding back. She wanted him to just take her.

But he didn't relinquish his restraint for one second. He kept kissing her. Kept touching her where she needed him most. Stirring, rousing, until she was almost out of her mind with desire, until she was moaning a song of need into his mouth, her body trembling beneath his, her nails clawing into his skin as she hurtled towards the peak. Finally he broke the passionate kiss, letting her gasp as the rest of her arched, utterly rigid in that unbearable moment before release. Oh, it was here. He'd pulled her through the burn and made her feel it. Her eyes closed, she cried out as the wave of pleasure hit, sweeping her away in that powerful turbulent crest. She clutched him fiercely as the sensations tumbled within her, drowning her in almost unendurable bliss. He pressed hard against her as she convulsed, not letting her pull back from the intensity he'd stirred. His fingers rubbed relentlessly, ensuring she received every last spasm of pleasure from her orgasm.

Finally she fell back on the desk, limp as the warmth spread along her veins, sending her into a lax, dazed state. Raggedly she gasped, trying to recover her mind, but it was impossible to catch her breath. Impossible to wipe the smile from her face. Impossible to believe what had just happened.

Never had a man made her feel so good. It wasn't just the orgasm, it was the heat and vitality he'd seemed to pour into her. He'd made her feel wholly alive, here and now. Twin tears escaped her closed eyes before she had the chance to brush them away but she was smiling at the same time, because it was so good and such a surprise and she was so happy.

Yet even now, despite that mind-blowing pleasure, the ache within burned anew. Suddenly she felt empty even with that elation still zinging around her. She wanted all of him. And she wanted him now.

Shocked at her surging hunger, she opened her eyes and looked into his.

'Antonio,' she whispered, shocked when she read what was so obvious in his unguarded expression. Torment—desolation and desperation. Feelings she understood all too well.

'Please.' She reached out to cup him—to make him feel as good as he'd made her feel. But he gripped her wrist and stopped her, his hand painfully tight.

'Don't touch me,' he ordered through clenched teeth.

His words hit like physical blows. It was utter, raw rejection.

She closed her eyes but his spurn had already slammed the lingering sense of pleasure from her. Emptiness ripped her open. Now their imbalance struck her forcefully. She was almost naked. He was fully clothed. She was vulnerable and exposed. He was sealed and silent.

But they were both angry.

He released her wrist, pulling away to put three feet of distance between them. He stopped and stood with his back to her, his hands on his hips, his head bowed. She could see the exertion in his breathing, as if he'd run a race to the death. He was trying to slow it, regulate it and recover his equilibrium. Well, so was she. But she was failing.

She sat up, yanking her top down to cover herself, confused and lonelier than ever. 'Maybe it's time—'

'I behaved like—' he interrupted her harshly, then broke off. He twisted to face her. Tall and proud and formal. Icy again. 'I behaved inexcusably,' he said in those remote, clipped tones. He bowed stiffly. 'I apologise.'

For a long moment she couldn't speak. Couldn't believe he'd become this remote statesman again. Did he feel guilty? Was he upset that he'd sullied the memory of his dead lover because he'd felt up the tart from the nightclub? Was that what this was?

Fury burned but oddly pity was entwined with it. She felt sorry for herself. Sorry for him. Sorry this whole moment had started.

But she only had to look at him to know any attempt at conversation would be futile. He'd scorched any sense of connection or compassion. There was simply nothing left. Yet he remained standing like a statue in the middle of her room, staring at her with that damned unreadable expression.

In the end she could only whisper, 'You behaved like a human.'

His nostrils flared but he didn't reply. He swiftly turned and strode to the door.

'You didn't want to be seen,' she called scornfully as this next rejection scalded her all over again.

He still didn't hesitate. He just walked out without a word, rapidly descending the stairs.

Bella closed her eyes until the sound of his footsteps receded completely. She understood anyway. He'd rather risk being seen leaving her club than staying another second in her company.

He didn't want to be near her ever again.

CHAPTER THREE

CARS ROARED: a relentless mass of humming metal and fuel. Distracted, Antonio almost forgot to applaud when the first passed the chequered flag. He'd not been looking at the finish line because she was down with the winning team's pit crew, and she was dressed not to be seen, but to stun.

Photographers called and clicked constantly, like seagulls incessantly circling a kid with an ice-cream cone. Bella paused long enough to send them a glittering smile, then turned to snap a selfie with the winner of the race. Doubtless she'd upload it once she'd filtered it to her satisfaction.

I don't need any man.

Her vehement denial replayed in his mind, but the vulnerability that the harsh-edged words revealed echoed loudest of all. Those tears after she'd come apart in his arms haunted him. He'd broken past that slick, sophisticated façade and found her to be tender and he'd been a jerk. Because he hadn't reciprocated. He hadn't been as honest with her as she'd been with him. And she'd been mortified.

But now, only hours later, her façade was back—beautiful and bulletproof. Grimly he fought the urge to take her somewhere isolated and break her walls down to get to that genuine, emotional response again. As if she'd allow him to now.

While he'd returned to the palace without detection that morning he was in no way pleased. He was a leader of not just an army, but a nation, and he never ran from a situation. Yet he'd run from the desire she'd aroused in him. Now regret and anger burned alongside it.

For the best part of a decade he'd staved off sexual want, using extreme exercise to gain self-control; his honed physique was a by-product of that intense discipline. Because he refused to hurt anyone the way he had Alessia and he refused to use women to satisfy purely physical desires. Discipline had become habit. It had almost become easy.

Until today.

Maybe his apparently uncontrollable desire for Bella had been a reaction to tiredness and stress. Or maybe it was because it had been so long since lust had burned him, it had been able to slip his leash like quicksilver…

He could come up with reasons, but they still didn't excuse his actions. And they didn't explain why he was unable to look away from her now.

She was ravishing, putting on a performance for more than the thousands in this crowd and her online audience of millions. This fortnight on San Felipe was packed with festivities and events, ones he had to attend while sandwiching in the vital trade talks and tax-exemption debates with the foreign politicians who'd come to work during the day and party at night.

Bella would use this fortnight to build her brand and define her club as the most 'it' venue on the island—if not the world. This was the reason for the glamour, the smiles and selfie-central behaviour. All those society events that he had to attend, she would be present at too. There would be no avoiding her. Not in the immediate future.

His jaw ached with the effort of holding back his frustration.

As soon as the race formalities had concluded, he returned to his large office in the palace. He listened to the requests of his aides, read through the official papers in the scarlet box on his desk and braced himself for the celebration reception that evening.

As he'd figured, she was there, draped in an emerald-green silk dress that skimmed her curves before falling in a dramatic swathe to the floor. He was even less talkative than usual, preferring not to circulate at all. It would hammer home his icy reputation even more, but so be it. If only Eduardo weren't away—his brother had more social patience. Antonio just wanted to get back to the paperwork and the important decisions.

Except that wasn't quite all he wanted.

He endured her presence three more times over the next two days. At a charity brunch, at the unveiling of the plans to redevelop the marina, at the opening night of the new exhibition in the national art gallery…

Every time he saw her, the craving bit harder.

He avoided speaking directly to her, but more than once he met her gaze. Across the crowd in the gallery, during speeches, every glance seared, stopping that breach in his armour from sealing shut again.

Three days since that morning in her office, he seethed at his inability to wrest back his self-control. His mind wandered every chance it got. When he should be focused, when he should be listening to someone else, when he should be thinking about things so much more important than himself, he thought about what he'd do to make her writhe in his arms until he heard her soft cry of release again.

That cry had made him harder and more wanting, yet more satisfied than he'd ever been in his life. He'd revelled in it for one incredible moment. Then he'd remembered. He couldn't have any kind of relationship.

Then he'd run.

But that cry had tormented his dreams day and night since. Now it was all he could think of.

He glanced at the valet pointlessly polishing Antonio's already buffed-to-brilliant shoes. He had a performance at the opera house to attend tonight and there was no way Bella Sanchez wouldn't be there.

'Leave me.' Abruptly he dismissed the man.

'Sir?' The servant looked nonplussed at the sudden command.

Varying from his schedule was impossible, given how crammed it was, but Antonio needed to pull himself together and cool this burn with a reality check. He needed to see *through* Bella Sanchez and remind himself she was merely a woman. And he'd refused hundreds, if not thousands of women. It was in their best interests that he had.

'I need ten minutes alone,' Antonio ordered.

His valet swiftly bowed and left. Antonio picked up the tablet he used to scan newspaper headlines. With a couple of swipes he opened up a video channel. The simplest of searches retrieved an endless list of clips. He clicked on the first. Lifted from a performance at one of the US's most prestigious ballet theatres, it had been viewed millions of times.

Bella Sanchez dancing the title role of Carmen. In this scene she was seducing a soldier to get him to do her bidding. Antonio watched, his gut tightening, as Bella sent the man a smouldering look over her shoulder—alluring, enthralling, *practised*. It was a move she performed on stage night after night after night, yet she made it utterly convincing. At the end of her solo the audience exploded, chanting her name over and over, stomping their feet, delaying the rest of the performance for a full five minutes while they called for encores. He stared at the screen, as spellbound as everyone in the audience had been, watching as she didn't break character for even a second. Haughtily she waited, accepting the adulation and keeping them in her sexual thrall as if it was only to be expected.

But when she'd lain before him, warm and exposed, she'd not been at all practised or polished. She'd been unrehearsed and real and what had happened had taken her by surprise as much as it had him. And the raw emotion in her eyes when he'd pulled away from her?

He'd hurt her. He regretted that. He regretted touching her.

Yet all he wanted was to do it again.

He tossed the tablet back onto the desk. Reduced to *watching* her like this, like some unbalanced stalker, was no way to find relief.

Why couldn't he end this aching awareness of her? The slow burn threatened to send him insane. He'd resisted already, hadn't he? He'd stopped before taking the pleasure he'd wanted so badly. He'd proven himself.

But he was tired of having to prove himself, tired of devoting every minute of his life to his crown. Maybe resisting had been the wrong action.

Why shouldn't he have something for himself for once? He'd been restrained for so long. Every other damn prince took lovers. His younger brother had been a total playboy. In other countries princes, politicians, people with power and wealth indulged their desires. Ordinary people did too. It was *normal.*

But not for Antonio.

Not when he knew the heartache the inevitable intense media coverage would cause. Nausea churned in his gut from guilt as he remembered. He was sure Alessia's parents knew the truth of what he'd done to their daughter. They never discussed it, but they knew. So the least he could do was protect and honour both them and the memory of her. It was his duty. Having a public affair with a woman like Bella Sanchez would destroy everything he'd worked so hard to maintain. And an affair *would* become public.

Slaking this haunting lust was impossible.

But still his blood burned.

At the theatre he saw her immediately. She'd made that unavoidable. A scarlet petal in a sea of black suits, she wore the colour of seduction and vampishness, unapologetically sensual and attention stealing and a bold choice given the red highlights in her hair. Held up by thin straps, her dress was cut low over her generous breasts, their size and shape accentuated by her slender waist. Her strappy sandals made her almost tall enough to look him in the eye. Except tonight she refused to look at him at all.

Her shoulders were very square, her spine ramrod straight, her chin lifted. She knew every single man in the audience was salivating over her. That was the point, was it not?

She was here to be noticed, coveted, prized, but not claimed. This was a costume. Which was the real Bella Sanchez—the cotton-pyjama-clad woman stretching before six in the morning, or this carefully made-up temptress?

His heart drummed a fast, heavy beat. He kept his hands at his sides and didn't even try to smile. Unfortunately she was seated in the box to the left of the stage. Of course she was—it meant everyone in the audience could see her. As the royal box was in the centre of the dress circle, he could still see her even as he stared hard at the stage.

A violinist performed a haunting adagio, a choir sang, a soprano dazzled. But it was when a couple performed a *pas de deux* in the first half that he caught the first reaction in Bella. He studied her closer and saw the heartache in her expression as she watched them dance—was that the sheen of tears glistening in those blue-green eyes?

The downturn of her mouth arrested his

heart. He gripped the armrests of his seat. He would not stand and go to her. He would not press his lips to hers. He couldn't let lust ignite again. But his imagination danced on, teasing him with the fantasy of her beneath him, smiling now as she looked up at him. How hot she'd feel, how she'd drink him in—

He gritted his teeth and glared back at the stage.

By the time the house lights came on for the interval she'd composed herself and was smiling again as she engaged with the city councillors she was seated with. The look she'd just sent one of them was straight from the stage. Antonio had seen it on that video clip only a couple of hours ago. It made sense. She'd spent most of her life studying how to entrance and entice and tell stories and emotions with her body. Her appearance tonight in the audience was just as much of a performance as any she'd done on stage. Just as he was performing as 'Prince Antonio' and masking the unruly battle swirling within.

He paced ahead of his aides, desperate to burn the energy building up inside, glancing at some of the other women present. They were as beautifully attired, but he felt nothing. It wasn't clothes, jewels, hair or make-up attracting him.

It was that indefinable, unique essence. *Lust.* He grimaced. Why couldn't he just shake it off?

A throng waited for him to receive them during the interval. He listened and asked a few courteous questions. He'd got through five guests when Bella walked in alone. A murmur rippled across the room as people reacted. The crowd parted, giving her a halo effect as she moved into the middle of it. She didn't look to where he stood at the farthest end, but he was certain she knew exactly where he was. Her 'not looking' was too deliberate.

Now the crowd's attention was divided—half watched him, half watched her. The flamboyant Spanish entrepreneur who'd financed her club scurried over to speak with her. But it was the wolfish man trying to manoeuvre his way towards Bella who snagged Antonio's full attention—and animosity. Jean Luc Giraud was a predator out to amass as much money, and seduce as many women, as possible. But the man barely got five paces before his path was stopped by another, equally predatory-looking male.

Antonio stilled and watched closely. The ability to communicate was vital to his work and long ago he'd learned to lip-read. It was a useful skill, never more so than now.

'Don't even bother.' The taller man blocked Jean Luc's path.

Antonio couldn't see Jean Luc's response, but the blocker was facing him, and every word was clearly drawled with arrogant laziness as he answered.

'She won't give you what you want.'

Antonio's gut clenched. He waited while Jean Luc responded. The blocker shook his head in mock pity.

'Go ahead and try. She'll flirt, but won't follow through.'

Jean Luc turned, enabling Antonio to see the last of his response.

'…a tease.'

'Exactly. Looks hot, but is colder than an icicle. When you get her alone she drops the act and refuses. She's a fake. Like her injury was fake. She couldn't handle the demands of the company. The second she got hurt she was out of there so she could become the club queen.'

Red mist momentarily fogged Antonio's vision, blinding him to whatever the asshole said next. That this fool had been lucky to kiss Bella and made such a muff of it that she'd shut down? That he'd not treated her how she ought to have been?

Once more he remembered her look of surprise when that passion exploded between them. How often had she *not* got the pleasure she should have?

Compassion burned at the injustice. Just because he didn't indulge didn't mean he thought others shouldn't, but it should *always* be good. Wasn't that the point? And if it wasn't any good, then of course she was going to say no. And the jerk here should just—

'Your Highness?'

He turned to the man beside him, forcing on a polite smile. 'Forgive me, I was thinking of something else.' He drew in a breath when he realised who had stepped up to speak with him. 'Salvatore.' He inclined his head, making a conscious effort to unclench his fists.

'You're enjoying the show?' Salvatore Accardi asked with an obsequious bow.

'It is nice to see families out enjoying themselves together celebrating the island.' Antonio faintly underlined the word *families*. 'I enjoy San Felipe's festival season very much.'

'As do I.' Salvatore smiled. 'I'm sure you remember my daughter Francesca.'

His *other* daughter. The legitimate one who was a few months older than Bella.

Antonio turned slightly. Francesca Accardi was taller than Bella, her hair a glossy brunette, her slim figure beautifully dressed. 'Of course.'

'It is an honour to be here tonight, Your Highness.' She smiled brightly. 'The performances have been amazing and I'm sure the rest of the concert will be as incredible.'

'I'm glad you are enjoying it.' Antonio bowed, about to step away.

But Francesca suddenly spoke again. 'My father's new boat came into the marina after the unveiling of the new plans this morning.'

'Francesca is a designer specialising in marine interiors,' Salvatore chimed. 'Graduated top in her year.'

'Congratulations,' Antonio replied with a nod to Francesca.

'You might like to see our latest beauty,' Salvatore added. 'Her work is very unique.'

'I'm sure it is spectacular,' Antonio answered guardedly.

Everyone knew he liked his boats—thought they were his one indulgence. But the truth was he liked them because he could work in peace without interruption.

'I thought the plans for the marina expansion were very interesting,' Francesca said. 'Overcrowding is a problem of course, but I've had some thoughts as to how it could be made more efficient…' She trailed off and smiled up at him.

Was this politicising or flirting?

Antonio figured boldness was a family trait, but he felt none of the stirring he felt in the presence of her fiery half-sister. He couldn't resist glancing over at Bella to see if the wolf jerk had made his way to her. But she stood alone, looking right back at him, her green eyes stormy and accusing, watching him talk pleasantries with the man who denied that her existence was his responsibility. As his gaze clashed with hers, she lifted her chin and she looked away without so much as a blink.

Anger bubbled. She'd deliberately blanked him. He wanted her to look at him, needing to understand that emotion in her eyes. Instead he wrenched his attention back to the woman beside him. Bella's supposed half-sister Francesca Accardi was watching him too closely. He flicked his fingers and the aide hovering nearby stepped up.

'This is Matteo,' he introduced him briefly. 'Matteo, I believe Ms Accardi has some interesting ideas on the marina development. I would like you to meet with her to discuss them.'

There was no mistaking the disappointment

in Salvatore's eyes as Antonio stepped back, leaving Matteo to arrange an appointment with Francesca. But Antonio was too used to people trying to make time with him, especially when accompanied by their single daughters. He turned back to spot Bella, but she'd vanished.

Bella sat in the plush seat in the exclusive box, one of the first to return for the second half of the variety performance. She'd intended to be one of the last—to maximise her exposure. As much as she loathed the tricks, she'd learned well from her mother. But her knees were now too wobbly to make that late entrance, her nerves too shredded from seeing Prince Antonio schmooze her father. The thing was, it was seeing Antonio that hurt more than Salvatore Accardi's customary rudeness.

Was she so stupidly weak she trembled at the mere sight of him?

Tonight she'd dressed with as much care as if she were still stepping onto a stage in front of thousands. She'd no shortage of glamorous dresses—people paid for her to wear their designs as long as she put her picture on social media. Getting the right look took longer than imaginable but it was a necessary part of the mystique and the 'lifestyle' her club was selling. Having lost her ballet career, she'd no other qualifications—*yet*—to call on. For all their fabulousness free dresses couldn't be eaten and she couldn't sell them for cash. If she ever did clear her wardrobe it could only be to raise money for charity.

So if she wanted to eat, she needed to earn real money from a real job, study on the side and eventually save enough to move on to what she really wanted to do. And as much as she hated her inherited 'notoriety', she needed it, because without it she'd have absolutely nothing and she had to work it hard now because it wasn't going to last—some other model or actress or lifestyle blogger would be the new flavour soon enough.

She had to be seen. Flirt if necessary. Dance in her own club. But most importantly she had to avoid the heartless Prince who'd judged and punished her so personally.

But deep down she knew she'd dressed tonight with him in mind. She'd felt his gaze on her at those other events since that morning and his attention—his disapproval—stung. She'd tried not to care that he'd left her so abruptly but she did. Too much.

She'd wanted more but he'd reacted with

such fury when she'd reached for him, he couldn't have made it clearer—she was so far beneath him.

And he was the ultimate jerk.

For a moment she'd actually thought they'd had a real kind of connection. He'd made her feel so good, then snatched it all away. She didn't know why but that one betrayal bit deeper than all the others she'd faced in her life.

She didn't enjoy the rest of the performance. She wanted to go and hide but she had to appear at the after-party backstage to show she wasn't down and out, had to smile at those she'd once danced alongside, knowing how they'd talked about her, and then had to go to her club and tirelessly work it up.

When the curtain finally fell she escaped her local council companions, telling them she'd meet them at the party shortly, but it was to the now empty stage she went rather than the powder room. Even with the curtain down, that vast black expanse felt like home to her, the one place she'd felt she truly belonged. Loneliness surged and she quickly ducked back into the wings before anyone saw her.

Pull it together.

She had her new kind of show to put on tonight.

'Bella?'

She whirled at the low whisper, blinking to get rid of the impending tears. How had he found her? Why was he alone?

'You're distressed.' Antonio stood stiffly at a short distance from her. In his black tuxedo he almost disappeared into the dark wings.

'I'm fine.' She tried to answer evenly, never wanting him to know how much she still hurt from his behaviour.

'Do not lie to me,' he said, very quiet and formal. 'Did somebody say something to upset you?'

'No one here could say anything to upset me,' she muttered, wishing it were true.

'No?' He held her captive with a mere look. 'I just told you not to lie to me.'

'Nobody has said anything to upset me. *Yet,*' she elaborated pointedly.

The scepticism remained in his eyes. 'Then what is it?'

She didn't answer—couldn't. He had no right to pry and he couldn't expect her to open up to him now just because he was asking in that gentle tone.

'Bella?' He remained standing so restrained a few paces from her, yet there was that huskiness in his voice.

'I miss it,' she replied quickly, as hushed as he, because it was easier to talk about her ballet than what was really upsetting her. 'I miss the moment when I'm waiting in the wings and I take a last deep breath and step forward.'

'You miss the applause?'

She sighed inwardly at that edge. Of *course* she damn well did. She'd been seeking approval from someone—*anyone*—all her life. And she'd never got it from those supposed to love her, so yes, she'd sought it from the masses. She loved that applause and she'd worked so hard to earn it. But she heard criticism in his voice and knew he'd never understand.

'I miss the freedom.' The stage was where she'd felt most comfortable. 'The feeling of being in control.'

'Control of what?'

'Myself. Knowing I can move the way I need to… That I'm as strong and as fast… That I've done the work and the world is at my feet.' She stiffened at the look in his eyes.

'So you're the one who doesn't like to lose control,' he said softly. 'And yet you did.'

Anger burned—swift and uncontrollable. 'And isn't that just what you wanted?' she snapped. 'To make a fool of me.' His rejection had been her ultimate humiliation.

And she wasn't letting it happen again.

She pulled up and tried to speak calmly. 'You'd better go before someone comes looking and sees you talking to me.'

But he walked towards her, not away. 'I want to talk to you.'

'You want to gloat? To crow over your victory?'

He halted barely an inch away. 'I don't feel like a winner.'

'You started. You stopped. You wanted to prove your power—'

'I wanted to please you. I wanted to see you pleasured,' he interrupted in a rough whisper. 'That is *all* I wanted. I wasn't thinking of anything else.'

The words, the way he said them, silenced her. A trickle of warmth worked down her spine. He'd *wanted* to please her? It hadn't been about making her pay?

Confused, she gazed at him. Passion smouldered in the backs of his eyes, but the way he stood so still was so *controlled*. Was that because his emotions were awry? Was that because he didn't trust himself?

'Don't you think I might have wanted to do

the same?' she whispered, unable to hold back even when she knew she ought.

'I *can't*.' The words were wrenched from him. His sharply drawn breath sliced into her.

'So you can give me pleasure but you can't receive it?' she asked, somehow feeling even more hurt than before. 'You punish yourself that much?'

A wild look flared in his expression. Her heart thundered but she refused to run; instead she stepped that last inch closer to stand toe to toe with him.

'That isn't it,' he muttered harshly.

'Then what is it?' she whispered, all caution lost. 'You don't like sex? Or just sex with me?'

She never talked back this way. She worked to keep men at arm's length, smiling and dancing but maintaining distance in a finely balanced art. But with Antonio she'd lost all that ability. For the first time in her life, she wanted a man to come closer.

He gripped her shoulders, leaning in to answer her. 'I haven't had sex in a long time. Thanks to you, it is all I can think of now.'

Satisfaction poured into her. Raw, feminine, sensual satisfaction. 'Then what stopped you?'

Why had he rejected her so brutally?

He didn't answer. He just looked at her. They

both knew she would have let him do anything. She'd almost begged. And he'd jerked away. That memory burned. She wanted him to burn too.

'You're scared you won't be any good after so long?' she taunted.

His laugh was short and unamused. 'Don't try to provoke me into proving everything to you again. It isn't necessary.'

He gazed into her eyes, then his focus lowered to her mouth. Her limbs weakened with that languorous feeling. The low ache that had been with her for days now sharpened. She wanted a kiss. Then she wanted *complete* satisfaction. It was only a millimetre away. One tiny decision.

'This situation is intolerable,' he snapped, pulling her flush against his lean, hard frame. 'We have to—'

'Bella? Is that you?'

She jumped, stepping back as Antonio released her at the exact same time. A quick glance at him showed sharp cheekbones and a clamped jaw.

Erik, her former ballet partner, stood just to the side of the wings. He was someone she counted as a friend, but he was the biggest gossip in the company. And with him—watching with eagle eyes?

Sebastian. Her blood iced. Of all the creeps she'd met in the world, Sebastian was one of the worst.

'I thought that was your dress...' Erik paused as he looked past her and saw who she was with. 'I'm awfully sorry. Are we interrupting?'

'Not at all. Ms Sanchez was kind enough to show me the stage on the way to the celebration,' Antonio answered with his customary quelling reserve, deflecting any suggestion of impropriety by demeanour alone.

For a split second Bella just gazed at him, amazed at his ability to revert to his formal 'prince' façade so quickly. And she now realised it *was* a façade. Why did he need such a remote, cold veneer? Did he never let anyone in?

He glanced at her, and she was shocked again to see that the heat had completely vanished from his eyes. A different expectation was within them now.

'Crown Prince Antonio, may I introduce you to Erik Lansing? He was the lead dancer tonight.' Bella obeyed Antonio's implicit order and acted as if nothing had happened. 'And this is Sebastian, the company's artistic director.'

Instinctively she straightened her spine as she faced her old boss. Sebastian had decided which ballerina got which part in each production. He was the man who'd assumed she'd be happy to become his lover, who'd been angered when she'd said no. She'd had to dance better than ever to prove her worth—to make it impossible for him to deny her the parts. But she could never shake that smoke of suspicion and innuendo amongst the other dancers. Sebastian had liked to let that smoke hang in the air, refusing to have it known she'd rejected him.

'I enjoyed your performance tonight.' Antonio grimly acknowledged the two men who'd almost caught him in a clinch with Bella.

He'd been a breath from kissing her. And if he had, he wouldn't have been stopping any time soon. Because she'd wanted it too. They'd have ignited the attraction sizzling between them and neither could have stopped until it had been fully assuaged.

He never should have followed her to the stage. But his curiosity—and desire—had been too strong. She fascinated him and he'd felt compelled to apologise and explain himself at least in part to her. Something he never did in a personal situation, because there *were* no personal situations. Until now.

But now he stood face to face with the 'blocker' who'd warned Jean Luc off Bella. This Sebastian slimeball was her old company's artistic director? That title meant power—over a ballerina in the company. Presumably he could offer promotion, or he could pass her over and give a prized part to another, more willing woman. Yet Bella hadn't given him what he'd wanted. And she stood straight, head held high, bracing herself in defiance in front of them all.

Antonio had known she had strength. Now he knew she had integrity too.

'Thank you.' Erik half bowed. 'I miss Bella though. I don't dance anywhere near as well with anyone else.'

He'd been Bella's ballet partner? Antonio watched as Erik slung his arm along her shoulders. Bella smiled at Erik but the look in her eyes wasn't the same as when she looked at Antonio. There was no desire, no anger, no passion. There was only a sorrow-tinged amusement. She didn't want the same thing from Erik as she wanted from him.

Even so, Antonio's stomach tightened. The jealousy was ridiculous. He was no better than any of the other predators in suits, sniffing around her.

'I must return to the other guests,' he clipped, his jaw aching. 'Excuse me.'

'Of course,' Bella murmured.

'We have to stay at this thing for at least twenty minutes, right? Then we're hitting your club.' Erik's voice carried as Antonio strode away. 'I hear it's full of beautiful young things.'

'Absolutely. Wait 'til you see my star barman.' Bella's laughter bubbled as she went back to her performance.

During the reception in the backstage lounge Antonio watched her execute those choreographed moves in real life again. But his bitterness receded when he saw that blankness in her eyes. It told him everything. This was an astute businesswoman doing what she deemed necessary to make her work a success. Beneath that determination, she had needs and desires that weren't being met.

So, thanks to her, did he.

An affair was impossible. But he wanted just one taste of the forbidden.

No one could know. And for that to happen, it could only happen the once.

Clandestine. Discreet. Finite.

There'd be no power games, threats or

sleazy rewards. They would just be two people working out an intense attraction on their own terms and in private.

Five minutes later he watched her leave with her entourage of dancers. She was deliberately breaking royal protocol and leaving the reception before he, the Crown Prince, did. Showing him she didn't give a damn.

Which might be true.

But she still wanted him.

CHAPTER FOUR

BELLA RECOGNISED THE man immediately. Prince Antonio's aide might be immaculately and discreetly attired, but he still didn't fit in. His expression was as austere as his employer's and he clearly wasn't at her club to dance.

She wasn't dancing either. She was playing the 'exclusive VIP room' card, trying to let Erik distract her, but not even his endless talk could keep her thoughts from one tall, dark and handsome prince for long. And now here was Antonio's errand boy at almost three in the morning looking as if he was on a mission. Her pulse sprinted, swiftly overtaking the fast-thudding beat of the club anthem blaring from the state-of-the-art speakers.

From her seat on the mezzanine floor she saw him identify her bar manager. She immediately rose, discreetly radioing for that manager to escort the aide to the small private office at the back of the bar. She went down via the curling steps in the main dance space, taking her time to smile with some of her guests so no one could suspect how on edge she'd suddenly become. There were too many people and every single one of them had a smart phone with a camera app.

After another few minutes working her way past the bar, she entered the small private room. He stood waiting in the middle of it.

'Ms Sanchez, my name is Matteo. I am Prince Antonio's assistant.' He half bowed as soon as she'd closed the door behind her. 'The Prince requests your company.' He held a thick white envelope out to her.

Her name was on the front, inked in a scrawling hand and underlined with a couple of heavy pressed lines that suggested urgency. Demand.

Bella.

Her blood ran faster. She could hear his voice, whispering her name as he touched her, devastating her defences until she'd melted in his arms. But he wasn't here now. He'd sent a messenger in the middle of the night. Had he even written her name himself?

'He requests my company right now?' she asked Matteo carefully.

'Apparently an issue has arisen,' Matteo answered, still offering the envelope.

Bella stared, unable to be sure that she'd heard innuendo in his tone or not, but his face was a blank mask. He'd learned from his master well.

'And this issue can't wait until morning?' she asked.

'If you would take the envelope, Ms Sanchez.'

She took it from him and turned it over, breaking the seal on the back. She drew out the single thick card and, with a cool glance at Matteo, turned away to read the note. But the card bore only two lines of that harsh writing.

We need to talk.

The bald statement was followed by a number and an address—she recognised it as an apartment building near her club and her pulse was *not* accelerating, but her breathing quickened. Her nerves tightened.

'I will escort you there now,' Matteo said, as if he were offering her the greatest service ever.

'That won't be necessary.' She put the card back into the envelope with care. 'I can't go there now.'

The surprise that flashed on his face gave her an inordinate sense of satisfaction.

'Prince Antonio requests your company,' Matteo repeated.

'So you said,' she answered, determined to stay cool. 'And I will get there when I can.'

'You don't understand—'

'I understand perfectly.' She smiled at him though her mouth felt dry as dust. 'You're the one who doesn't understand and nor does he, obviously. I have a business to run. So you can tell him that I'll get there if and when I can.'

Matteo didn't reply but she wasn't bothered by his scrutiny. She wasn't afraid of him. But she was wary of how Antonio made her feel—and how much she wanted him.

'If you'll excuse me, I need to get back to my guests.' She clutched the envelope and left him to find his own way out.

But she didn't return to her guests. She climbed all the way to her own tiny apartment at the top. She put the card on her desk—the one he'd kissed her on—and stared at it.

Was this how a prince made a booty call? With just her name, an address and a lame 'we need to talk'? Did he do this all the time? Send his aide to set up shag-a-thons for him in a private apartment in town so no one would ever know?

So much for the myth of heartbroken, isolated Prince Antonio. Turned out the supposedly heroic, self-sacrificing Prince of the People had feet of clay. He just wanted it like any other guy. On the side when it convenienced him.

She was livid. And she was ignoring him.

She went back down to the dance floor. She wasn't going to drop everything at his beck and call. But she couldn't concentrate properly. Time crawled. It felt like hours until four a.m. finally struck—yet it was only forty-five minutes since Matteo had left.

It was another hour before her staff had gone and she'd locked up and could shower. The cascading hot water didn't ease her tension any. Sleep wasn't happening. So she dressed in skinny jeans, a light tee and ballet flats on her feet.

It was five-thirty in the morning when she finally made her move. She'd go and see him and tell him to his face.

No.

She wouldn't be his latest secret lover.

She walked out of the side door, ensuring the alarm was enabled, and saw Matteo leaning against the doorway of the building opposite. He crossed the street to where she stood.

'I will escort you there now,' he said.

'Have you been waiting here all this time?'

He nodded and turned in the direction of the apartment.

'You don't need to—' She started to argue but realised the poor man was only following orders. She was better to save her fight for facing Antonio. She started walking, pretending not to care that Matteo remained a half pace behind her the entire way. Clearly he *was* used to doing this kind of errand for his boss.

Fury pushed her faster.

At the apartment building the security guard wordlessly opened the door, not looking Bella in the eye. Matteo stepped in front and led her to the elevator.

Yeah, he'd definitely done this many times before.

He entered the lift only long enough to punch in a code at the keypad. It whooshed up swiftly, leaving her feeling as if her stomach were still on the ground. Ruefully she reckoned her brain was back at her club.

When the elevator stopped on the top floor she stepped out. The heavy door on the small landing was open. Antonio stood, resting a shoulder against the frame, staring at her. He still wore the jet-black tux, the jacket immaculate and tie neatly fastened; only the hint of shadow on his chiselled jaw gave away the passage of time—that and his glare. Serious, handsome, smouldering, he said so much in silence.

Too bad. She lifted her chin, because his rejection still *hurt*. 'You summoned. I came.'

She walked past him into the apartment, commanding the centre space.

'What do you want from me?' Years of training stood her in good stead; she knew how to fake confidence 'til she made it.

Antonio quietly closed the door, taking a moment to temper his response. She'd kept him waiting, he'd had zero sleep, and he didn't have the patience for endless debating. This was one situation in which action would speak louder than words.

But he needed the words because they meant he'd retain control. Of himself, of what was to happen, of how this would end.

And he wanted to hear her speak too. He liked her challenging edge, as if she wasn't going to agree to everything he had to say. At least, not immediately.

'Would you like to sit down?' He gestured to the plush armchair rather than the wide sofa. Enforcing social niceties at this moment would help keep him civilised.

'I'm not going to jump just because you said to.'

Her reply shredded the remnants of all polite pretence, exposing the sensual tension. Combustion was a breath away.

He gave up on civility and crossed the room to tower over her. 'And yet here you are.'

He'd known sending Matteo had been a mistake. His brother Eduardo had relied on Matteo for his discretion and reliability. Antonio had never had cause to before and should've known it would be better to do a job himself. He should've waited until later and gone to her club alone. Yet he liked this look in her eyes—baleful anger bubbling over sensual awareness.

'What do you want from me?' she repeated unevenly. 'You want me to dance for you?' She rolled her shoulders and took a half-step to the side.

It was barely a dance, more a suggestive movement, but Antonio was unable to answer. Another emotion entered her eye—determination, then *calculation*.

She moved ever so slightly while her gaze

remained locked on his. There wasn't the freedom he'd seen when she'd not known he was watching her alone in the club. She looked every bit as beautiful, but he saw her self-awareness, her moves made for their intended effect on her audience.

On *him*.

'No,' he snapped.

Instantly she stopped. Her sultry mask fell, revealing her anger in full, making her all the more stunning.

'Not like that,' he added. 'I don't want to *watch*. I don't want a *performance* from you.'

'Then what do you want?' she flared. 'To humiliate me again?'

'Humiliate you?' His own anger ignited. He'd never intended to do that and he was furious he had. He grabbed her hips and hauled her against him. 'I want what we had. I want the real thing.'

He crushed her mouth under his, unable to contain himself a second longer. Energy radiated from her—resistance, anger, but most of all desire. In the next moment she melted, opening, pressing closer. Then she kissed him back—*hard*.

This was what he wanted. Her unrestrained reaction to him—negative and positive and the total eroticism that burst to life the second they touched. All the resistance within her transformed to passion. She burrowed closer, angrily clutching his jacket.

He lost his head in her heat. He ached to rip them free of their clothing. Have her exactly as he wanted—bared and welcoming with that fire-gilded hair tumbling free about her shoulders and her body hot and slick.

But he pulled away, brutally breaking the kiss because he had to put restraints around this. And he was damn well ensuring she had more than a quick, angry orgasm this time. He'd see her fully sated. Fully his.

Breathing hard, he held her at a distance, taking primitive pleasure in how long it took for her to regain her balance and stand on her own.

'This cannot go on.' He'd give in to lust, but only once.

'What?' she asked. Fury combusting, she shoved his hands from her shoulders.

'It only worsens with time,' he said quickly, before she continued to think he didn't want to resolve this in a way they'd both appreciate. He could hardly bear to look at the luminescent need in her gleaming green eyes; he couldn't resist her ferocity. 'We have to work this out.'

It had only been a few days, but Bella knew what he meant. The hunger, desire, and the *frustration*. The emotions he roused in her were the most intense of her life.

'So you sent your errand boy to make your booty call.' It was anger and arousal coursing through her veins now, a heady combination that made it almost impossible to think. She *felt* too much.

'I didn't want to attract attention,' he explained crisply. 'It wouldn't be good for either of us.'

'The publicity would be good for me,' she argued hotly, pushing forward what she knew would be his greatest objection to anything happening between them. Just because she could. 'Make my club even more popular. I could do with that success.'

'They would drag *you* through the mud and you know it. Don't act vapid. I know you care more than that.'

'Do you?' How could he really know anything about her?

He cupped her chin and tilted her face to his, capturing her gaze in his steely one again. 'I saw you. I felt you. You're more vulnerable than you wish to admit.'

Ever so lightly he touched the tips of his fingers to the pulse beating frantically just below her jaw. Not a threat, but a caress of concern.

Her heart stuttered. 'I don't need your protection. I can handle anything.' She jerked her head, forcing him to release her. 'It's your name you're worried about. Having an affair with me would ruin perfect Prince Antonio's holier-than-thou reputation.'

'I don't care what others think about me,' he said softly. 'But there are other people who would be hurt by my personal life becoming public. Discretion is necessary because it is kind.'

Silenced, she gazed up at him, her heart melting. He wanted to be kind? He wanted to protect people other than the two of them. She couldn't help but wonder who they were.

'And you do not want to be hunted any more than you already are.' His gaze narrowed, penetrating. 'You do not want to be treated the way your mother was. You do not want to have every detail of your life reported on. Invented. You do not want to have your ex-lovers paid fortunes to tell your sexual secrets. They would stop at nothing to get that information should you be known to be my lover.'

He hit precisely where she was most vulnerable. She never wanted to live the way her mother had. And yes, while she courted publicity now, it was one thing to manage her own media relations and give them enough to keep them interested but not have them hound her completely. But the way they would pry if they knew she was having an affair with Prince Antonio?

It would be unbearable.

'Yet you're still willing to take the risk?' she asked.

'I am talking only one night.'

Just once.

So this would never become an affair. It would be nothing more than a one-night stand. And there wasn't even much of this night left.

'I don't want to fight it any more,' he said ruefully. 'The last few days have been hell.'

That he felt as intensely as she did soothed her some.

'No one will ever know,' he added.

'Except you sent your man to fetch me at three in the morning in a club full of people,' she pointed out.

'I trust him with my life,' Antonio said.

'Because he's done this for you so many times before?' Maybe that shouldn't bother her, but it did.

'Never for me,' Antonio answered solemnly. 'But I cannot answer for my brother.'

Relief seeped into her stiffness. Prince Eduardo had been 'the Playboy Prince'. Of course.

'You do not need a man. A husband. A hero,' Antonio said quietly continuing his persuasion. 'You are determined to be independent. I respect that. But you want…' He paused. 'I have duty and obligations. I will never marry because I can never give a woman all she deserves. But I, too, want…'

'Do you?' She was somehow hurt, despite knowing everything that he said was true. 'But you don't have lovers. Or is that just the publicity line?'

'It's not just a line,' he said quietly.

She rested her palm on his chest, daring to intrude where she really had no right. Just to see if he could be honest with her. If he could share when only a few days ago he couldn't share anything. 'How long?'

'A long, long time. I've been busy. After a while it wasn't something that was important to me.' A glimmer of laughter suddenly lit his face. 'But don't worry, it won't be over too quickly.'

His ability to pleasure her was the last thing she was worried about. He'd already given her the best orgasm of her life, and proven his personal restraint at the same time. 'Why now, why me?'

That serious, brooding look returned. 'Because I can't think of anything *but* you. Because I'm tired of trying to fight it already. I know it's the same for you. I come near and your body reacts. You can't help the way you respond to me.' Unflinching, he demanded equal honesty from her. 'Do you have a lover currently?'

'Do you think I would be here if I did?'

'Of course not. I apologise.' His expression softened. 'There is more talk about you than actual action.'

'Does it matter?'

'No. But do you think I don't know how much of the Bella Sanchez "story" is made up?'

'You don't want to know the truth?' She straightened, determined to defend her scarlet honour even when really she'd never been that 'scarlet'.

'I know it already. You give yourself away every time I touch you. Every time I come near you. You react differently to me.' He put his hands on her waist and drew her closer. 'You cannot hide how you react to me.'

'That's not fair,' she said huskily. 'As if you're all that experienced.'

He laughed appreciatively. 'I might be rusty, but I'm not ignorant. And you're not the sophisticated vamp you try to portray.'

If this was him 'rusty' then heaven help her when he hit his stride.

He ran his hand up and down her spine, partly soothing, mostly arousing. Every touch seemed designed to torment her.

'The other morning…' He paused and looked at her with concern. 'I saw you. I felt you. What happened, how I made you feel… was more than you expected.'

She flushed, embarrassed that he'd known her orgasm had come as a surprise.

'I want to make you feel that good again.' Intent darkened his eyes.

'It's not wise.' But her body yearned for it.

'Because I made you emotional?'

'You were too.'

He froze for a moment; his hands stopped those teasing touches. 'I like being able to make you feel good. And you do want me to kiss you again.' Deliberately, lightly he rubbed his finger across her lip. 'And I want to. Everywhere.' He suddenly pulled her hips against his. Hard. Letting her know exactly where else he intended to use his mouth.

'You always get what you want?' she asked breathlessly, the feel of his body against hers was so good. The promise in his eyes exquisite torment.

'I'm the Crown Prince—most people are pleased to do things for me.'

'So I should feel honoured?'

He shook her gently then pulled her to rest against him again. 'Stop trying to stall and just admit you feel the same.'

'The same?' She stiffened, trying to hold back the desire threatening to overwhelm her. Did he really feel this as intensely as she? Did he want her the way she wanted him this second?

'I like how good you make me feel,' he muttered.

'I didn't do anything. You wouldn't let me.' She'd been so hurt by that.

A wry smile curved his lips. 'You need me to prove it? Again. Untrusting creature.'

'Do you blame me?' she asked. 'You ask me to admit things when you rejected me so harshly. You wouldn't let me near you. You made me—' She broke off. 'And then you left. You couldn't get away quickly enough.'

His smile faded. 'I apologise. You took me by surprise. You were right and I was wrong. I shouldn't have walked out and I have regretted it every second since.'

'You're the Penitent Prince?' She couldn't breathe.

'I want you more than I've ever wanted anyone. I wouldn't be here now if I didn't.'

At his words that last little knot of anger disintegrated within her.

'Nor would I.' But she shivered because somehow his admission made *her* feel vulnerable.

He slid his hand beneath the hem of her thin tee, tracing his fingers up her spine. His touch warm and firm.

'Chemistry like this… I didn't think it happened,' she confessed.

'Nor did I.'

It was just physical, right?

'You don't like it,' she muttered, her thoughts derailed by the swirling pattern he was drawing over her skin with his fingertips.

'It's a distraction,' he answered evasively. He slid his hand up to cup the nape of her neck and pushed her back over his arm so her shirt pulled taut. He gazed down at the way the fabric rubbed against her nipples, emphasising their hard outline.

'So you think if we have what we want, then we'll no longer want it?' She arched uncontrollably against him as he sucked one tight nipple into his mouth, bra and tee and all.

'Yes.' He bent to give her other breast the same sinfully good treatment. 'This cannot be anything more than here and now. You wouldn't want it to be anything more.'

She arched against him again, unable to resist rocking her hips against his hard pelvis. He was right. She didn't want any of what would come with this if it became public. 'Will you allow me to touch you this time?'

'I don't know how I got the strength to stop you. I don't know how I walked away,' he muttered. 'I want to see you naked.' His glittering gaze raked down her body, felt like a force—drawing heat from her, making her want to move in a way she'd never wanted before.

'We each take off one layer at a time,' she suggested. 'It's only fair.'

'Life isn't fair.' He smiled wolfishly and pushed her tee shirt up.

'*This* time, it is going to be fair.' She demanded it.

He didn't answer, but there was a glint in his eye as he straightened her up, stood back and held out his arms, letting her peel the perfectly tailored jacket from his shoulders. Slowly, savouring the moment, she tugged his tie free, then unbuttoned the pearl buttons of his starched white shirt.

'That's more than one layer already,' he noted, his breath stirring her hair as she moved in close.

She didn't care. She was too busy exposing his chest. Heat balled low in her belly. He was gorgeous. Nothing but lean muscle and bronzed skin and a faint line of dark hair arrowing down the centre of his rigid abs to his belt. For the first time she took real pleasure in just looking. And then kissing. Then touching.

She traced over his ridged muscles. 'You're beautiful.'

'That's a word to describe you, not me.'

'You exercise.' She unfastened his belt and fumbled with his fly.

He moved to help her, toeing out of his shoes before shoving down both his dress pants, his briefs and socks until he straightened and stood utterly bared before her. 'Every morning.'

She stared, her mouth dry as she gazed on his honed, immaculate body. His regime had to be intense to be this fit—as if he ran or swam for long periods at a time. 'You're disciplined.'

'I have to be. I have a lot to do.'

And he was going to use that discipline and self-control with her now; she could see the intent in his eyes.

'You keep everything contained in its place,' she muttered. Work, exercise, sleep. She was in the sex box for him. And that was just fine.

So fine.

Except her heart was thudding and there was an ache within her that had never been there before.

'You're the same.' He lifted her tee, and she wriggled to help him. He unclasped her bra and briefly cupped her full breasts in his hands before moving to tug her trousers down. 'You're sleek, strong.'

'It makes me feel better if I've moved.' She nodded, lifting one leg, then the other, so he could take her panties off too.

In that they were a match—both physically driven, both worked hard. Both couldn't afford this messiness, but now they were both naked.

She licked her lips. She wanted everything all at once, but she didn't know where to start.

'Bella.' He muttered her name harshly and

stepped forward, pulling her into his arms to French-kiss her senseless.

They kissed, touched, kissed again until she was all but delirious and weak-kneed. But then he dropped to his knees and pressed his mouth to her *there*.

She gasped his name.

'I can't wait to hear you,' he muttered approvingly. 'Again and again.'

Oh, no, this wasn't happening that way. Not again. She pulled back and fell to her knees too. 'I want to hear *you*,' she said.

But he was stronger. He lifted and laid her down on her back and moved between her splayed thighs. 'I can't keep my hands off you. Or my mouth.' He moved down her body, trapping her hands at her sides as he licked and kissed from her navel, to her most intimate curve where she was embarrassingly wet already. Then he rose onto his knees to study how he'd spread her beneath him. 'I want to taste you as you come again. Now.'

That devilishly sexy look in his eyes almost sent her over the edge then and there. But she didn't want to come before him. Not this time.

'I want *you* to enjoy it,' she moaned as he ran his hand over her breasts, gently cupping, then teasing.

'You think I didn't?' He shook his head and stroked her again with his skilful fingers. 'There's no greater feeling than knowing I've pleased you.'

'It's the same for me.' She arched uncontrollably as his hands worked further south. 'Can't you understand that?'

'I do.' He bent to her again and kissed her most sensitive nub. 'You can please me, right now. Come for me, Bella. Let me taste it.'

His tongue was so wicked there was no way she couldn't. Groaning, she ran her hands through his thick hair, holding him to her as he pleasured her with his mouth and hands. She rocked as she rode the crest of her orgasm, no longer embarrassed about how wet she must be, because the way his fingers were thrusting was so divine and the words of approval and pleasure tumbling from his wicked mouth were making her orgasm last longer than she'd have thought possible.

He cradled her as she recovered, small aftershocks making her quiver every so often. The pleased expression in his eyes called forth her own competitive spirit.

'My turn.' Suddenly energised, she rolled and moved onto all fours.

'Turn?'

'To taste.' She slapped her hand in the centre of his chest and pushed, making him stay where he was, flat on the floor.

'Bella—'

'Don't argue with me,' she said fiercely. 'Don't deny me. Not this time.'

But he cupped the nape of her neck and drew her down to him, kissing her deeply. Almost she submitted completely to the desire to simply roll back and let him do whatever he wished with her. But she needed this. Wanted it.

She pulled away and looked into his eyes. 'I'm going to kiss you,' she said. 'Everywhere.'

He didn't answer, but nor did he stop her. She took her time discovering his body. He was strong, but sensitive too and she took pleasure in teasing out those secret spots. What he liked. Where he liked. His neck. His nipples. His thighs.

And slowly she honed in on his enormous erection. Licking her lips, she glanced up at him to gauge his reaction as she moved, curling her hand around the thick base of him.

'Bella…'

She utterly disobeyed the implicit order and opened her mouth to draw him in.

'Bella.'

There was no ignoring him that time.

She released him to glance up into his stormy eyes. 'Please.'

For a long moment he held her gaze, his expression strained. She realised he was holding his breath.

Then he sighed and an almost tender light entered his eyes. 'I'm the one who should be saying please.'

Almost shyly she smiled at him. Then she looked back down at his straining erection. The single, glossy bead at the tip of his shaft told her he was close. Feminine pleasure flooded her. She wanted to taste all of it.

She heard his long hiss as she took him as deep as she could into her mouth. She sucked hard as she pulled back, and she rubbed and took him deep again. Oh, she loved to rub him. Loved to lick and suck and feel every powerful tremble she could pull from him.

She didn't stop. Rubbing, kissing, sucking, she lost herself in her rhythm, in the pleasure of touching him. His hips bucked, bumping her as she straddled his thighs. She shivered at the power beneath her. His legs were so strong, she couldn't wait to feel the full force of his lovemaking.

As his breathing grew harsher, she gazed up

the length of his body. His skin gleamed from a sheen of sweat. His arms were outstretched to the sides; she could see the veins popping as he grasped at the plush carpet beneath him. Every muscle in his body was strained as he tried to hold back. She didn't want him to hold back.

'I'm going to drink every last drop.' She smiled with carnal promise. 'I'm going to watch and taste and feel you as I make you come.'

His muttered oath was mostly indecipherable but it made her smile deepen. Then she returned to him. He was so beautiful and all she wanted was to make him—

'Bella!'

His shout echoed in her ears, so filled with raw relief that she felt as if she were riding that crest with him. As the spasms eased she kept sucking him as deep as she could, holding true to her words and loving it as he shook beneath her.

'Bella.' He released a long breath and his body went lax. 'Bella, Bella, Bella.'

Still astride him, she sat up and looked down his length to his handsome face, tracing her fingers down her neck, between her breasts and to her belly, following the heated path of his seed within her. She felt so femininely sensual. And so aroused.

With shadowed eyes he stared back up at her.

Undaunted, knowing he too was finally sated, she smiled.

Swiftly he sat up and flipped her. She was flat on her back and he was pressing her hard into the plush carpet, kissing her breathless before she could blink. His fingers were between her legs and he made a guttural sound in the back of his throat as he felt how wet and ready she was. She writhed, riding his hand for a moment, so unbelievably pleased.

'Temptress,' he muttered and nipped her lips with his teeth.

He shifted onto his knees, reaching beyond for his trousers on the floor near them. In a second he was ripping open the foil package and rolling the condom on.

She lifted up onto her elbows, in awe of his already rigid erection. He glanced over and caught her staring. He smiled, but she read the determination in his eyes, felt the dynamism in his tense body as he covered her, and knew her moment of dominance was past. He was back in control. He was going to make her pay and it was going to be a heavenly price.

'I don't know how gentle I can keep this,' he muttered, stroking her intimately again. His eyes widened as he felt her body's reaction to his words. 'You don't want gentle?'

'I just want you in me,' she muttered low and harsh and hungry, unable to hold back her darkest desires. She wanted him too much. Only he had made her feel this way. And if she only had him this once, then she was holding nothing back. 'As deep and as hard as you can.'

He kissed her. His tongue lashed the cavern of her mouth with exactly the kind of fierce strokes she was aching for.

For the first time in her life she truly wanted passion.

'You have a hot, sweet mouth and a hot, sweet body.' He looked into her eyes as his fingers probed her wet arousal. 'But you don't want it all that sweet.'

She whimpered at his tormenting rubbing. But he was right.

'Answer me,' he commanded, pushing fractionally deeper and then pulling out.

She moaned in disappointment. 'Yes,' she admitted, aching for his return. For *all* of him.

'You want it hard.'

'Yes.'

'Fast.'

'Yes.'

'Now.'

'Yes.' Her head fell back as her blood burned. She writhed under him, desperate to assuage the ache so deep within her. 'I want you in me. Please.'

He nudged her thighs further apart with his knee and settled over her. He was so hard, so masculine and he smelt so good and she could feel him, almost there.

Never had she wanted a man like this.

She held her breath as she stared into his gorgeous pale blue eyes. She saw the determined fire in them and wanted to be consumed in it. She saw his jaw lock. Then he pushed forward.

'Oh, yes.' She tensed, locking him in as an orgasm rolled over her in a sharp burst of ecstasy. 'Oh, yessssss.'

Her breath shuddered in the shock of it. He was finally there and he felt so good. She moaned again, convulsing in pleasure.

'What are you doing coming so quick?' He smiled tightly down at her as she gasped for breath. His expression was teasing. But strained too.

She didn't know. She'd never come during penetration before, let alone that quickly. But the amazing thing was, she wasn't far off coming again.

'What are you doing not moving?' she moaned breathlessly, stunned that she was on the edge again. If only he'd move. If only he'd give her everything. Oh, God, she never wanted this to end.

'Enjoying the view. You're so beautiful like this. I could watch you come all day.'

She shifted, wrapping her leg around his lower back, trying to pull him deeper.

'Don't tease.' She stroked his face and whispered what she wanted most of all. 'I want you to come with me. In me.'

'Oh, hell. Bella,' he muttered hoarsely. His wicked smile faded as he gazed at her. 'Then you might want to hold on, sweetheart.'

But he held onto her, sliding his hands under her back and gripping her shoulders to keep her with him as he pressed forward, deepening his possession of her.

Her breath hissed as he pushed to the hilt. She met his gaze and knew she was in the eye of the storm. Hurricane Antonio was about to hit.

'Please,' she asked one more time. She wanted it all.

At last he moved, pulling back only to grind

into her. Hard and deep he drilled into her, again and again and again. And it was so good. She met him thrust for thrust. Energy sizzled between them; their ride suddenly became frantic and wild. Their sweat-slicked bodies banged faster and faster.

'So good, so good,' she muttered over and over and over.

But then she could only moan in mindless pleasure each time he drove deeper. It was so carnal and so physical and so good. She kissed him everywhere she could with honest, unchecked abandonment. This wasn't sweet, this was decadently sensual and she had to curl her fingers into his muscled flesh to hang on as he forced his pace faster still.

'Come with me, Bella,' he commanded harshly, then kissed her.

His kiss held so much passion, it felt as if he were pouring his very soul into her. She felt him shaking against her even as he drove deeper still.

She arched, every muscle in her body straining. Her breaths were high-pitched moans as he pushed her nearer and nearer to that peak. She heard his breathing roughen, felt the rigidity in his whole body and revelled in it.

'Yes!' She managed to lock her arms around

his back, fiercely holding him to her as she shattered beneath and about him, her screams unchecked and raw as that intense sensual tension exploded.

She heard him groan her name, then his hoarse growl of intense pleasure as he thrust one last time, releasing long and hard into her.

When she could think again, she found he'd eased off her and was lying on his side facing her. Her heart thudded.

This time when he grabbed her wrist it was not to reject her. It was not to push her away. It was to demand the exact opposite.

'More,' he grated, his expression untamed. 'More now.' His passion was utterly off the leash now. 'You should have come as soon as you got my card.'

'I couldn't.' And she couldn't be more sorry about it.

'There is not enough time.' He moved over her, his body hard again. 'We didn't even make it to the damned bed.'

'This is all the time there is.' She parted her legs wider to accommodate his muscular strength. 'This is all there can be.'

She saw his reaction at the remembrance. Duty before desire.

'Then we'd better make the most of it,' he said, his jaw tight, his eyes savage.

His determination made her hot. His intensity made her tremble.

It was slower that time. And silent. There were not the hot, wickedly teasing words to start. He was careful not to bruise where she was most tender. But his gentleness was such exquisite torture. He made her feel so good tears welled in her eyes as she squeezed her muscles tight to lock him in place. She didn't want this to end. She didn't want him to stop holding her, looking at her. Didn't want him to stop ensuring she was out of her mind with pleasure. He could make her feel such unutterable, exquisite pleasure. She embraced him with all the fervour she could, yearning to return that favour. That was when it grew wild again. Loud and physical and fast.

But finally they lay slumped together, utterly spent. Silent again.

This time he was the first to move. This time he didn't meet her gaze. This time really was the end.

Quietly, carefully he left her, disappearing into another room. She sat up, curling her legs up and wrapping her arm around her knees. Dazed, she took in the discarded mess of clothing. He was right, they hadn't even made it from the lounge floor they'd been so eager and hurried. And it was all over already. Bittersweet melancholy filled her.

He walked back into the lounge. He'd swiftly dressed in jeans and a tee shirt. They might be casual wear for him, but he'd slipped back behind his reserve.

She wanted to kiss him. She wanted to fall back onto the floor and take him with her. She wanted that delicious feeling all over again. But she didn't dare.

'I am sorry, I must leave.' He glanced at his watch, his thoughts clearly elsewhere. 'I'm late already.'

'Of course.'

'Stay and sleep,' he instructed politely. 'The bed is through there…' He had the grace to look slightly sheepish.

'No, I have things I need to do as well.' She pulled her clothes nearer. 'I'll leave ten minutes after you. Will use a different exit from the building or something.'

He was silent. 'I would like Matteo to ensure you get home safely.'

That poor guy was still in the building ready for service? 'That's not necessary.' Her skin burned anew with that all-over body-blush and she quickly pulled her tee shirt on, not bothering with her bra first. She just wanted to cover up. She just wanted him to leave already.

His jaw tightened but he didn't argue. He stood for another moment and she inwardly winced at the awkwardness.

'Goodbye,' he said stiffly, still frowning at her, looking as if he might say something more.

She didn't want him to.

'Goodbye, Prince Antonio.' She lifted her chin and threw him her most sophisticated 'Bella Sanchez' smile. 'It was a pleasure.'

CHAPTER FIVE

IT WAS ENOUGH. It *had* to be enough because he didn't deserve the pleasure she could give him and she didn't deserve the pain he would inevitably give her. He had to retain his control. She was out of bounds now. Once was a calculated risk. Once more could only be a disaster.

Antonio walked past the line-up of guests, greeting them as he went, determined to be as focused as ever. He was almost halfway through the continuous schedule of event after event in the festival fortnight. He'd been spared her presence at some occasions. But not this one. At his request she'd been sent an invitation and she had not refused. She was not stupid.

She wore a black dress that revealed nothing yet managed to imply everything. Her loose hair shone, the reddish strands glinting like threads of fire under the chandeliers. She stole his breath. And that was before she smiled. Or spoke.

If she spoke, he'd be lost.

But his desire for her wasn't the reason why he'd ensured she attend this particular function. It was in *her* interest to attend. It wasn't that he was desperate to see her again. He was simply helping her out, because he was in the position to be able to.

Salvatore Accardi was also a guest at this late afternoon's drinks, yet Antonio noticed the man didn't say hello to Bella. He was her father, Antonio was in no doubt of that, yet he didn't even acknowledge her presence with the politeness you'd afford a stranger. He acted as if she weren't there. Beyond rude.

But Bella was working the room with that bulletproof style of hers, refusing to let her father's ostracism daunt her. Antonio felt like cheering her. He understood social isolation and he didn't want her to feel the sharp edge of it. She'd done nothing to deserve it. He'd checked her out. Beyond that super-seductive façade, there was nothing. She'd not been caught lying or stealing or cheating...she was a woman—that was all. A woman who couldn't help who her parents were. A woman he still wanted.

He caught Matteo's eye.

'Ensure she's not left alone,' Antonio instructed as the aide came over. 'There are people here it would benefit her to meet and people who might give her a hard time.'

And then he decided to set the example for everyone. He deliberately walked over to talk to her; it would be too obvious if he didn't and he refused to be anything like her father.

'It is always a pleasure, Ms Sanchez.'

She didn't immediately reply but her eyes narrowed on him.

She wasn't appreciative of his efforts?

His focus changed, arrowing on the electricity arcing between them. He'd made a mistake. He'd thought he'd be lost if she spoke to him, but, really, it had taken only one look.

'It seems you have guests from every sector of San Felipe society here tonight,' Bella murmured, trying to regulate her racing pulse, but seeing him threw her balance completely. 'Business leaders, rally drivers, retired politicians…' Her voice trailed off. 'Even me.'

Antonio almost smiled. 'Why shouldn't you be here?'

'You know very well why.' She shifted, restless because of his nearness. 'You shouldn't have invited me. Our agreement was once only.'

She'd been a fool to think once would've been enough. The last few days since had been horrendous. And this invitation? It hadn't been in his hurried scrawl. It had been formal, printed and distant, yet she'd not hesitated for a second. The craving to see him had been too great. She'd applied her lipstick with a shaking hand, she'd been so full of anticipation. Now he was right with her and holding herself back was almost impossible.

But she hadn't slept properly in weeks because she'd been getting the club ready and now it was open she was frantically busy and the sleeplessness was affecting her more each day. So she didn't have the energy to build her defences; she couldn't control her own heated trembling.

'That wasn't why I invited you,' he answered impassively.

Bella's blood iced. It wasn't? Didn't he want her again? Had that one morning truly been enough for him?

'This is a reception for San Felipe's most successful local business leaders,' he continued with his customary distance. 'You are a businesswoman who's carving out a brand and a service that has seen unprecedented success already. That's why you're here.'

Rejection and bitterness bruised. 'To network with people who don't want my business in their town because I'm some kind of bad influence?' she asked acidly.

Salvatore Accardi had been sending hostile waves across the room since she'd walked in.

She curled her suddenly cold hands into fists. She wanted to leave. To escape Antonio more than anything.

'It's not like you're running a brothel,' Antonio drawled softly enough so only she heard. 'Entertainment is a large part of what San Felipe offers and you're drawing in large numbers of younger customers. We don't want the island to be famous for being the holiday destination of only the old and wealthy.'

'It's never been that. The old and wealthy men have always had their young and beautiful companions with them on San Felipe,' she mocked.

That was what her mother had been for Salvatore Accardi—the nubile young accessory. And in recent years with the two Princes in charge? Beautiful and ambitious and hopeful women had been visiting in droves. Bella was just giving them a place to display themselves.

Antonio's eyes gleamed but then he glanced over her shoulder and his expression became as remote as ever.

'You are not out of place here.' He bowed formally. 'I hope you enjoy your evening.'

That was *it*? No heat? No words with hidden meaning or secret smile? Nothing. Disappointment deepened as he walked away.

It *was* all over for him.

Well, she wasn't letting him see how that hurt. She'd stay, she'd 'schmooze' and show both Salvatore and Antonio she was made of stronger stuff than either of them realised.

To her surprise it wasn't dreadful. People talked to her. Complimented her on her past career and asked about the club. She became aware of Salvatore Accardi talking loudly on the other side of the room about the degeneration of inner-city San Felipe, but she wasn't going to engage. She knew people were watching.

Antonio was watching. But he needn't worry, she wasn't going to cause a scene. Despite what he thought, she'd not chosen to set up her business in San Felipe so she could exact some kind of patricidal revenge on Salvatore. Life wasn't that simple. She'd come here because it was the one place she could. And it was the one place she actually enjoyed being, other than the stage.

But Salvatore Accardi's voice was drowned out when a ruddy-cheeked older man arrived late and walked straight over to Prince Antonio and greeted him with an etiquette-breaching booming voice.

'Please pass on my congratulations to your brother Prince Eduardo on the birth of his daughter,' the man gushed loudly as he beamed at Antonio.

'Thank you.' Antonio nodded intently, seeming aware of the sudden interest from all those standing near. He lifted his head and spoke clearly. 'It is very exciting for us. I am informed she's very determined to maintain her own schedule and refuses to fall in with her parents' request that she sleep at *night*.' He paused as everyone chuckled, a small smile lightening his features. 'So I am confident she will make a wonderfully stubborn Crown Princess in the future.'

There was the tiniest silence before a woman ventured another question.

'Will we get to meet the little Princess soon?'

Antonio's expression tightened and he paused before replying. 'Princess Sapphire is very young and this time in her life is very precious and private for her parents. I'm sure you'll all agree.' He softened his words with another glimmer of that rare smile and absolutely everyone in the vicinity completely agreed.

But Bella watched as that small smile faded from his eyes and her heart smote. With masterful PR skills, he'd offered just a hint of something personal about the new baby Princess to satisfy public curiosity while protecting her privacy. But at the same time his words had underlined his own abdication from any family or personal life of his own. He had no intention or desire to marry and provide an heir of his own. His niece would one day take the throne.

Until then he would be alone. Because he was the Heartbroken Prince.

Her heart thumping unaccountably quickly, Bella turned towards a waiter to ask for a glass of sparkling water. But as she turned her gaze hit upon the man who didn't just deny his role in her existence, but who'd chosen to denigrate and torment her mother *and* her.

Salvatore Accardi was looking right at her with such undisguised loathing she stumbled.

Her lungs malfunctioned. She straightened but couldn't turn away.

Salvatore Accardi could. With a final condescending appraisal, he muttered something indecipherable to the person next to him and deliberately turned his back on her.

It was the most public of rejections and yet probably—hopefully—no one would have noticed.

Except *she'd* noticed and she was so humiliated that not even years of experience controlling her emotions as she faced huge crowds could help her stop the blush from spreading like a sudden rash over her skin. She glanced at others in the group, unable to resist the curiosity—had anyone seen?

The person who stood next to Salvatore, a tall brunette, was staring. Her half-sister. Francesca. Beautiful and—with the way she too then turned her back—every inch her father's daughter.

Bella finally found the power to move. She walked almost blindly from the room. She didn't want to talk business and she definitely didn't want to banter or flirt or *be* Bella.

'Ms Sanchez.'

Bella blinked and paused. Matteo had materialised beside her looking bland, but he spoke with gentle courtesy.

'I thought I would introduce you to Tomas Mancini. He owns the island's most popular Michelin-starred restaurant here on San Felipe. He owns several others too, in mainland Europe.'

His lengthy explanation gave her a chance to breathe and as he slowly walked her to the other end of the vast reception room she had time to pull herself together properly.

Tomas was about seventy, accompanied by his elegant wife, also around seventy years old, and they were both charming, both talkative and standing with them was somehow soothing. She stood with her back to the rest of the room, relieved of feeling the pressure of vindictive, prying eyes.

'Tomas started out as a firefighter, you know. He was based at the station you have refurbished as your club,' Tomas' wife, Maria, informed her. 'That's when I met him. He rescued me, you know.'

'Did he?' Bella was diverted. 'From a fire?'

'A fire *alarm*. There was no danger but I was mortified.' Maria nodded in all seriousness. 'But I like to think of young people having fun there now.' She paused for a second then added quietly, 'I had fun there once.'

There was nothing in her tone, but Bella looked sharply into the older woman's eyes. There was the veriest hint of a wink. Bella finally smiled.

'Maria, Carlo has just arrived.' Tomas turned to Bella. 'He was our first chef who moved to an outer island to open a satellite restaurant for us last year. Would you like to join us?'

'Thank you, I will shortly,' she said, wanting to give them a chance to have some time alone with their friend. 'I'll freshen up first and then find you.'

'If you'll accompany me, I'll show you the way.' Matteo stepped alongside her again.

Bella glanced at him in surprise; she'd thought he'd been called away.

'Thank you,' she said, quietly appreciative of the way he walked between her and the group that Salvatore and Francesca stood in. Salvatore's voice still carried; she couldn't hear the words but just the tone oozed arrogance.

'It is in here.' Matteo paused by a discreet door out in the long corridor.

Bella stepped inside, drawing in a deep breath, but as she closed the door behind her someone loomed right in front of her. Just as she was about to scream she realised who it was.

'You gave me such a *fright*.' She clapped her hand on her chest, almost needing to thump it to get her heart started again.

Antonio stood a breath away, his customary reserved expression incinerated by the raw need in his eyes. But he said nothing.

Now her hurt heart raced—sending anticipation and hunger sparking around every one of her cells.

'What are you doing in here?' She licked her dried lips and watched that need in his eyes burn all the more intensely.

'I need to see you again. Alone. Tonight.'

Relief hit her like a tornado, blowing the roof off her tension. She released her breath in a shaky sigh. But just as relief hit, so did the impossibility of what he was saying. 'We *can't*—'

'Not now, no,' he agreed. But that didn't stop him taking the step nearer so he could pull her against him.

His hand smoothed down her back, as if he were trying to soothe her, but she felt the rigidity of his body and realised how tightly *he* was coiled. She rested her head against his shoulder, stifling her groan of sheer relief.

'I'm sorry I used Matteo again,' he muttered against her hair. 'But there are too many people—'

'It's okay,' she interrupted. 'I understand.'

She understood he was lonely and that for whatever reason he wanted *her* to help him find physical release. That was okay; she wanted him for the same.

They were both hurt and lonely.

She placed her hand on his chest and looked up at him, willing to accept however it had to be, as long as it could happen again. Just the once more.

'Bella.'

She barely had a chance to hear his strained mutter before his lips were on hers.

Passion burst free at first chance. She wrapped her arms around his neck, wriggling closer for more heavenly contact. His arms tightened, lifting her clear off her feet, and she moaned. She never wanted this kiss to end. Always he made her feel so good, filling her with that incomparable bliss. Dangerously addictive and too good to deny. She rocked against him, using her body to blatantly offer him everything. Right here. Right now. She was beyond caring.

'Bella, we can't,' he muttered.

'We can,' she pleaded. 'Just quickly. So quick.'

He touched her, growling between his teeth as he felt her readiness. 'Without protection?'

She bit back her own moan and vehemently shook her head. 'You think I'd ever make the same mistake as my mother? Contraception is covered.'

He stared at her another second and then crushed her mouth with his. The kiss was nothing but raw frustration. But then he tore from her—lifting his head to look down at her, holding her in place so she couldn't rub against him any more. She felt his tension morphing back to that impenetrable self-control. He had no intention of having his way with her here and now.

The disappointment was appallingly deep. Again.

'I've missed you,' he said.

She melted. His completely. But she made herself pull back and stand on her own two feet. 'I'd better get back out there,' she replied, determined to be as strong as he.

'You'd better redo your lipstick first,' he replied, flashing a wicked smile.

'And you'd better remove it.' She eyed his pristine white collar meaningfully. 'Before you end up wearing more.'

His hands loosened from her waist and he stepped further into the beautiful powder room, allowing her space. 'I'm sorry Salvatore Accardi is here tonight. He is too loud.'

Bella shrugged as she opened up her small evening purse and stepped forward to check her make-up in the gold-framed mirror. Her fingers shook.

'Does he ever talk to you?' Antonio watched her carefully restore the glossy sheen to her lips.

'He only talks *about* me.' She grimaced at her reflection. 'He thinks all I want is money from him.'

'And do you?'

She turned and sent him a sharp glance. 'I'd rather starve.'

'I saw him look at you. Then blank you,' Antonio said.

Embarrassment burned through her again and she turned away, wishing Antonio couldn't still see her face in the mirror. 'The most cordial we've been in years.'

'Don't try to make light of it.'

'He doesn't hurt me.'

'Don't lie to me,' he said softly. 'Go ahead and give him a hard time. Just don't make a mess.'

She added a last swipe of gloss. 'I'm not here to give him a hard time. I want nothing to do with him. I don't care what he thinks or says or does.'

Antonio was silent a moment. 'I will make arrangements for tonight.'

She put her lipstick back in her small purse and then turned. 'I will deal only with you and Matteo. No one else.' But she would give him that.

'Thank you.' He cupped her face and gazed down at her for a long moment, as if reading her thoughts. But he resisted her silent request to kiss her again.

'I must go now,' he said apologetically and then swiftly left the room via another door.

Bella turned back to her reflection and tried to think calm thoughts to reduce the telltale colour in her cheeks. But flickers of excitement shot through her veins. She wanted him again. Couldn't and wouldn't say no to him or herself.

Maybe that made her his concubine. But

she would take nothing else from him. Not a penny, a dress or a jewel, not a thing. And she was not his friend. Only his lover. And only for one more night.

CHAPTER SIX

THE HOURS THAT night stretched for ever. For the first time since she'd opened the club, she couldn't wait to close it. As soon as she'd seen off the last of her employees, she stood in the doorway. It was still dark, but in another hour or so the sky would lighten and the sun rise. A black car slowly cruised down the street towards her. Unmarked but opulent, it pulled in just by the main door, parking illegally. The driver's tinted window wound down a couple of inches. She'd expected Matteo, but it was Antonio.

Quickly she stepped forward and got into the passenger seat. He pulled away in seconds. She couldn't help but glance along the street, nervous that someone would have seen them. But the road was empty.

Silently he steered towards the very heart of San Felipe.

'You can actually drive?' She tried to make conversation with a tease, but her throat was dry and her voice tight.

'I am allowed, occasionally,' he replied in his formal way, but then he smiled. 'Ready?'

The giant gate before them opened without him hitting a button. She didn't see any guards or any officials as she stepped out in the internal garage that was bigger than the average-sized house and was filled with eye-wateringly expensive cars.

'This is the palace.' She whispered the obvious as he led her into the wide hallway. Even with the dim night lighting she could see the gilt-edged paintings lining the walls, the pedestals with priceless sculptures and the glass cabinets filled with antiquities and artefacts.

Her heart hammered. She'd never expected him to bring her to the palace. Wasn't it too risky?

The imposing building was incredibly silent and huge and she was paranoid there were security cameras everywhere snapping her with him.

'I know,' he whispered back. 'I want the comfort of my own bed.'

'But—'

'Be quiet.' He turned and quickly kissed her for emphasis. 'Someone might hear,' he whispered, then took her hand and led her through the maze.

Surprised, she glanced at him and saw the mischievous grin on his face.

He was Antonio, the ultra-serious Crown Prince, wasn't he? He owned this oversized, unbelievably opulent place and yet here he was sneaking around like a teenager.

He led her up some stairs, then more stairs and long corridors and finally came to a set of doors on the third or fourth floor—she'd lost count. He opened them and hung back to let her walk in first.

'This is your private apartment?' she asked, knowing the answer anyway, but feeling as if she needed to say *something*.

When he'd closed the doors she turned to face him. But that gorgeous, elusive smile had faded and his expression was even more closed off than usual. Did he feel as awkward as she?

'When did you last have a…guest up here?' she asked.

That brought his smile back but he remained silent.

'You're just trying to make me feel special,' she joked lightly.

'You are special.'

She walked around the large room, mainly to hide the blush she could feel heating her cheeks. He didn't mean anything by it, but the gentle flirt was nice.

His apartment was a masterpiece of elegant understatement, the decor minimalist compared to the multitude of treasures in the cabinets lining the corridors. But it was so impersonal it made her heart ache for him again. Even she, with few truly personal possessions, had put her own stamp on her room. She had the flowers she loved to get from the early morning market, she had a small print from Paris to remind her of happier times with her mother, she had the ballerina jewellery box she'd won in her first ballet competition when she was barely five and had treasured ever since. But Antonio had a beautifully styled masculine lounge with nothing obviously personal that she could note. There were no paintings on the walls and no photos at all—not of him and his family and none of Alessia—which relieved her in one way, yet saddened her in another.

She turned to face him again and found he'd

been slowly following her. Now he was only a pace away.

'You want to see all my rooms?' he asked, something veiled in his expression.

'I want to see everything,' she replied before thinking. She was so much more curious than she ought to be.

'There's not really that much to see.'

Well, there was beauty and incredible design and craftsmanship, but she wasn't here to admire an art gallery and she didn't want to treat him or his home as a museum exhibit. That was what his life must be like all the time and she wanted to understand more about him.

That was when she realised his place didn't matter; it was the *person* before her who held all the clues. If she wanted to understand him at all, she needed only to spend time with him. But they had only now. She gazed into his unfathomable eyes and wished she knew how to make him smile.

'I thought you wanted to see everything?' he finally prompted her.

'No.' She shook her head. 'Now I just want...' Her words faltered.

He took the last step towards her. 'Me.'

She nodded. 'Just you.'

She wanted to focus wholly on him, but they weren't here to talk. This was a clandestine convenience. A risky, stolen moment. Her heart tripped and thudded too fast. She waited, anticipating that burst of passion. They probably still wouldn't make it to his bed.

But he didn't kiss her. He took her by the hand. 'Let me show you one thing.' He walked down the hallway and opened the furthest door, waiting for her to walk in ahead of him.

'What's in here?' She summoned a tease. 'Your hidden den of iniquity?'

She walked in without waiting for an answer and stopped in surprise.

The room was large, its floor-to-ceiling windows protected by billowing drapes, protecting his privacy yet allowing the citrus-scented summer air to perfume the room. It was all but empty. Bella drank in the large expanse of polished wooden floor. And in the corner was a baby grand piano.

'You have your own dance studio?' That floor was begging to be danced on.

'Music room,' he corrected with a laugh.

'You're a musician?' She turned to look at him.

'You're surprised.' His rare smile flashed and stayed.

'You never seem to do anything other than serious "prince" things.'

'I appreciate many things. But especially music.' He walked over to the piano. 'It relaxes me. As dancing relaxes you.'

She was delighted to discover this and that he'd shared it with her. And she wanted him to share more. 'So will you play for me?'

He raised his brows at her.

'Please.'

'It would be my pleasure.' He sat down at the stool.

Bella crossed the floor and rested her hand on the smooth, glossy wood of the piano. It was beautiful to touch and she bet it would be an amazing sound. He glanced up at her for a moment then looked down to the keys. Intrigued, Bella leaned closer.

He began. After only a moment, Bella froze, unsure of how to react. He'd chosen an elementary piece and was literally banging it out. Two fingers smashed down on the wrong notes. He hit so *many* wrong notes, and it was so loud, Bella didn't know where to look. But then a wicked smile spread over his face and his hand positioning changed. The melody changed. *Everything* changed.

'You tease.' She laughed, relieved, and

moved closer to watch. He shifted on the piano stool, straightening.

'The look on your face.' He chuckled as he played, beautifully.

'Who knew solemn Prince Antonio would be a prankster?' She leaned over his shoulder, letting her hair brush against his cheek, aiming to distract him and make him hit a wrong note for real this time.

'You didn't know what to say.' He stopped playing and reached up to hold her in place near him, turning his head to press a kiss to her cheek. 'I was lowering your expectations. Now you think I'm better than I actually am…'

She pulled back to read his expression. 'My assessment of your performance matters to you that much?' She never would have thought he'd care.

'I've never played for anyone else.' He shrugged and glanced back to the black and white keys.

'I'm honoured.' And she was touched, that warmth in her soul that he'd let her into his secret life, just a little.

'Dance for me,' he softly requested as he began another piece. 'The way you were that morning I spied on you.'

'Okay.' Her heat soaring, she kissed *his* cheek in the lightest of caresses and stepped away from the piano. 'Barefoot, okay?' She kicked off her shoes.

'Don't feel the need to stop there.' He sent her a wicked look. 'Naked would be amazing.'

She laughed, pleased at his emerging playfulness. 'I never dance this way for just anyone, you know.'

He nodded, all seriousness again. 'I do know.'

She laughed again at the arrogance implicit in his reply but her heart fluttered, enjoying the lightness and liberty to just *be* with him.

He'd chosen a romantic melody and it was so easy to let go and lose herself in the streaming beauty of it. Smiling, she stretched her arms wide and simply moved, not showing any fancy steps, not needing to prove anything to him.

That was the thing, with him—physically, at least, she could simply enjoy the sensations, the moment. And now, the music.

But as the melody worked towards its crescendo she couldn't help looking at him to gauge his reaction. Her gaze meshed with his and was caught fast. His magnetism pulled her nearer. As the music grew softer, she danced closer. Softer and closer still until, as the last note died away, she slipped between the piano and him. He leaned back to let her straddle his muscular thighs. That wicked smile curved his lips and he began to play another piece, a teasing glint warming his ice-blue eyes.

She decided two could tease. She bent close and poured all the radiance she felt into her kiss. The notes of the piano continued to sound for only a moment. Then his magic fingers began to play her and she was so very glad she'd worn a dress.

He slipped the soft fabric up her thighs, exposing her to his touch. She wriggled and he slipped the silk right over her head.

'Antonio,' she breathed softly, so hot for him already.

'At your service,' he promised, leaning forward to kiss the crest of her breasts. 'I'm wondering if I can make you sound as good as my piano.'

'Play me and see.'

'I can already see,' he muttered in a pleased tone.

She felt his hardness beneath her and ached to free him from his clothing. She reached for him.

'Nu huh.' He shifted her above him with a laugh. 'I'm playing you, remember?'

'I was going for some harmony. Accompaniment.' She needed him with her. In her. Like now.

'Soon.' He soothed her with a kiss.

'No. Now.' She kissed him hard.

But he was ruthless. Relentless. He caressed, kissed, rubbed. Hard then soft, changing his stroke and rhythm, tormenting her until she banged the damn piano keys herself, trying to hurry him to get him to take her. When he finally relented and let her reach her release, she screamed long and loud until she slumped into his arms with a sigh.

'I can't take any more,' she begged. 'I need you. Please.'

He clasped her tightly and carried her through to another room. He set her on her feet and stood back from her.

'Take me, then,' he invited.

She noticed nothing at all about his bedroom. She was only focused on him. But he had to help her strip him out of his clothes. She was too frantic, too needy to get her fingers to work properly.

'Condoms. Pocket,' he muttered roughly.

She retrieved one and with a small smile set about ensuring he was sheathed. She took her time and used her mouth as much as her hands and when she'd finally finished he was swearing in a continuous stream beneath his breath.

She laughed and pushed him so he fell back on the bed. But the moment she knelt on the expansive mattress to join him he moved, as quick and powerful as a panther catching his prey. She rolled, letting him, welcoming him. She couldn't wait a second longer anyway.

'Hurry,' she called to him. 'Please.'

But he paused and smiled down at her and she knew what that wicked, gleaming smile meant.

Sheer, delightful torture.

'You're not going to do this fast, are you?' She shivered as her body geared up for more of his teasing onslaught.

He angled his head as if considering the plea in her words. 'It might end up that way. Eventually.'

She licked her lips and ran her hand down his rock-hard abs. 'I'm willing to fight dirty.' She'd do whatever she could to make him claim her sooner rather than later.

That challenge sharpened the edge in his expression. 'Go ahead, darling, do your worst. I intend to fight dirtier.'

Oh, Lord, she was in trouble. She yelped in laughter as he tugged her further up the mattress so he could claim the part of her most begging for his attention again.

And then she just gave in to his desire to see her soar again. He might be reserved, but when he was fully focused on *her*—it was wicked heaven.

That magical hour later she smiled as he lay sprawled, sweat slicked and breathless, at the opposite end of the bed. The coverings were on the floor, the dawn light warmed the room and she'd never been as relaxed in her life. And she'd never felt as close to anyone else either. Not just physically, but it was as if she was in tune with him and they'd made the most beautiful music together.

He rested his head on his hand and ran a finger along the jagged red scar than ran down her shin and to her ankle. 'Does it hurt?'

'No. It just tickles,' she murmured.

'What happened?'

'Glass in my shoe.' She stretched her foot languorously, unutterably relaxed.

He frowned. 'Glass?'

'In my pointe shoe,' she explained briefly. 'Not much. I didn't feel it until I was partway through the performance. But, you know, the show must go on.'

He shifted down to her foot and inspected her toes.

'Don't.' She tried to curl them away because they were so ugly and now she was self-conscious and regretted telling him that much.

'You kept dancing?' He released her foot and she pulled her legs from his reach.

'Of course. When you're in the zone, you feel invincible. You don't notice until it's almost too late. At first I thought it was just a bad blister or something. In the end I fell and landed badly and broke my ankle and shin.'

And when she'd looked later, there'd been blood seeping through her pointe shoe. The cut had been so deep it had severed nerves and the chunk of glass they'd struggled to remove had been viciously jagged.

'The show went on.' She shrugged, playing it down with a casual smile. 'The understudy stepped up. I went to hospital.'

One of the pins they'd put in was still there and during those months in plaster she'd lost flexibility, muscle tone. Confidence.

Everything.

'There was no way you could build up your strength again?' he asked. 'Retrain and get back out there?'

'Not to the level I want.' And it had been ruined for her. That someone in her own company had hated her that much to do something so horrific?

She'd thought the company had been her safe haven but she'd been wrong.

So she was determined to be independent now. Any success she had, she would own in its entirety. She wouldn't be vulnerable by being reliant on anyone else. She had to control her own destiny and haul herself out of any problems alone. It was the lesson her mother had never learned.

'How did the glass get in your shoe?' Antonio asked ominously.

She didn't want to answer but she knew that look in his eye. The wickedness had vanished and he was in 'ruthless ruler' mode. She shouldn't have answered so thoughtlessly in the first place. 'I guess some people didn't believe I deserved my position in the company. That I was there because of my profile, not talent. Sex appeal, not technique.'

He looked grim. 'Did they catch whoever did it?'

'I didn't want to cause a scandal and nor did company management.' Sebastian had asked her not to go to the police, arguing bad press would destroy the company. And she'd had her reasons for agreeing with his request.

'What?'

She flinched at the fury in Antonio's tone.

'I didn't want people to know I was a victim,' she defended herself hotly. 'I didn't want the world to know I had enemies who'd do something that mean. I didn't want to show that.' She hadn't wanted *anyone* to know how vulnerable she was. How isolated. So she'd left and played up the party queen. 'I fell. My leg broke. End of story.'

And she'd trust no one now. Not even a prince.

She reached out and ran her hand over the small silver elephant that she noticed sitting on the nightstand, wanting to distract them both. 'This is pretty.'

He glanced at the trinket, still frowning. 'Alessia gave it to me for my birthday.'

Silently she wondered which birthday, how long ago and what significance the elephant held. All she knew about elephants was that supposedly they never forgot anything.

Maybe that was what it was—for him to remember her. They'd been school sweethearts for years before getting engaged, hadn't they? Bella returned the trinket to the table and looked back down the bed to Antonio.

His expression had shut down, of course. Remote, reserved Prince Antonio had returned. He might be lying at her feet, but he couldn't be further removed and it couldn't be more obvious that he didn't want to discuss it with her. Of course he didn't.

That sense of intimacy she'd felt only moments before—that closeness beyond the physical—dissolved. He'd never let her into his life the way he'd let his fiancée. He'd never love like that again. He wouldn't let himself. And that was fair enough. She too knew how much it was possible to hurt.

She smiled, determined not to let it show that *she* hurt right now. She was the distraction, the secret lover, the light relief for the royal workaholic. And she'd keep this private and fun because *he* was her distraction too. He was the one man who'd finally made her feel *good* and enjoy her sensuality and she wasn't going to let anything ruin this last stolen moment she had with him. Certainly not any stupidly weak emotion.

But how did she forbid her heart from falling for him?

CHAPTER SEVEN

THE HOURS AND days stretched ahead, empty and frustrating, loaded with meetings from European delegations and civic duties. Nothing he could get out of.

He'd certainly been unable to decline this afternoon's invitation to tour the new addition to the cancer unit at the hospital. While there, the staff had taken him on a tour of Alessia's Garden. Amongst the beautiful roses and serene seating in the heart of the hospital grounds, he'd given his speech and thanked the committee for all the fundraising they'd done over the years, and continued to do, in his fiancée's name. Because of them her name lived on.

They didn't know that because of him, she'd died.

Not even his brother knew the truth.

Desperation curled around him as he read through the next day's timetable. He needed a break from it. For the first time since he'd been crowned he wanted a holiday and an escape from the weight he carried on his shoulders. He'd never had more than a few days away and even then he'd taken work with him. It had been the one constant in his life, the one thing he knew he *could* do right. It was his calling.

But now he craved another moment of escape—from duty, from his past, from the lie he lived day in and out.

He didn't deserve it, but he hungered for a moment of selfishness—the time to laze, linger and laugh on a bed with Bella instead of stealing a too-quick liaison in the last hour of the night.

He wanted just a little more. A whole night. A whole day. Enough of a feast to cure him and help him forget.

Three days since he'd done the unthinkable and brought her home, he sat alone in the palace, watching the hands of the clock slowly tick by.

There was no escape from his unrelenting schedule. And even if there was, he couldn't go to the island: his brother, Eduardo, was there.

Eduardo.

The brother to whom he'd never told the truth. The brother who'd repeatedly asked him how he could serve him better. The brother who'd changed so much in the last year since finding happiness with his soldier wife.

Antonio stared at his desk and finally picked up his phone. His brother answered immediately.

'I need you to come to San Felipe,' Antonio said quietly. 'I need you to attend a couple of events for me.'

'You're not well?' The shock in Eduardo's voice burned.

'I'm fine.' He couldn't lie about that. 'I only need a day or so out.'

'I will come right away,' Eduardo answered, still obviously stunned, but he didn't question more.

'Thank you.' Antonio rubbed the back of his neck. 'It's nothing serious. I just need a little time.'

'It's fine. I'm glad you asked.' Eduardo sounded as if he was moving already. 'If I need to make contact—'

'I'll be on the water.' Antonio gazed out of the window to the inky black space where the Mediterranean ebbed and flowed. 'You can radio me on the boat.'

Because he wasn't completely reckless. But nor could he wait 'til dawn.

An hour later he stood in the landing just outside her office, looking over the narrow balcony railing to where she was in the middle of the dance floor. It had been a risk, but at this hour the club was mostly in darkness, the lights flashing, confusing, disguising.

Everyone present was too busy noticing her to notice him anyway. In white trousers and a slim white top she danced in the centre of the main floor. There was a space around her, like a halo, as if somehow everyone knew they were forbidden to get too close.

But they watched. They *all* watched. And Antonio watched as Matteo told her. She stiffened and swiftly walked off the dance floor. Antonio stepped back into her office, anticipating.

'You shouldn't be here,' she said, striding in only moments later and slamming the door behind her.

'And yet here I am.' And he couldn't help but be aroused and amused as he drank in her energy. This was exactly what he wanted. Bella looking strong and fierce and crackling with fire.

'This is my club.'

'This is my country.' He crossed his arms, forcing himself to wait for her comeback.

'And you want to be seen here?'

'I thought this was the place to be seen. Am I going to inhibit your guests' pleasure?'

'They'll be thrilled to be in your presence. I'm sure they'll bust out their best moves for you. Especially our female guests. Will you be joining them on the dance floor or just *watching*?' Her eyes glinted.

He breathed in carefully, cooling his blood. But he was looking forward to the next twenty-four hours too damn much. It was all he could do not to reach for her now but if he did that, they'd never leave.

'Or is this another snap compliance inspection?' Bella smirked.

'Actually, this is an abduction.' He smiled back, hugely appreciating her not so subtle bite.

Her eyes widened. 'I'm sorry?'

'I'm taking you with me.'

'Pardon?'

'You don't need to pack. We're leaving now.'

'I can't leave *now*.'

Satisfaction thrummed. It was only timing she was concerned with? She wanted to come with him. 'Either you come quietly and right away, or I have the whole place shut down.'

Her gaze met his. Her face flamed at the double entendre he'd intended. He shifted on his feet, releasing the tension that was streaming through his body.

'Nothing like abuse of power, Antonio,' she finally responded.

'I have your best interests at heart.'

'Really.'

'Seriously.' He admired her independence but it irritated the hell out of him at the same time. 'We can leave quietly. Everyone is interested in the other celebrities on the dance floor.'

'Getting good at plotting, aren't you?'

'You look tired.' He frowned, because she did. And she looked paler than usual.

'Way to make me feel attractive.'

'When did you last get to bed before midnight?' he asked.

'What concern is it of yours?' She shook her head at him. 'You're not supposed to start caring, Antonio. That's not what you're about.'

It wasn't about *caring*. It was about having a very little more time for just the two of them. 'You work too hard and sleep too little.'

'So do you.' She shrugged. 'But that's not the point. It's no business of yours and I am not here waiting for your beck and call. I don't live for your summons. I have my own life to get on with.'

'Yes, you're right.' Every word she spoke was true. But there was something else equally true. He strolled up to her, framing her face in his hands and tilting her head so he could see right into her eyes. 'But you want this as much as I do.'

Her expression altered, the defiance drained and disappointment brought those shadows back.

'What I want doesn't really matter, though,' she admitted, a hint of sadness colouring her soft tone. 'I can't leave.' She gestured to her laptop open on her desk. 'Because I need to run the business. I need to understand it. I'm more than the face for it. I need to be the brains behind it. I need to make it work.'

Bella wasn't about to admit it, but Antonio was right: she was so tired and in need of a break. And that he was *here*, that he'd come to her once more?

That stunned her. Delighted her. *Distracted* her.

But if she could stay focused for just a little while she could pull her life back on track, *without* relying on anyone else. No one was taking her career from her again. No one was taking anything. 'I can't go with you.'

His eyes lasered into her, branding her even

as she tried to resist him. She lifted her chin. It wasn't her problem if he didn't like hearing the word 'no' for the first time in his life. But after a moment her heart starting skipping.

'Don't look at me like that,' she whispered.

'Like what?'

'You know.' She shook her head. 'It's not fair.'

His smile appeared. 'You look at me like that.'

Her resistance wavered. 'Antonio, please,' she asked, determined not to let him dictate her world in this way. She needed to keep this on her own terms. She *wasn't* a plaything—for all that manufactured media representation. She had concrete goals and she had to meet them. He couldn't derail her long-term plans. 'Don't make me change my mind.'

But she was tempted. And he knew it.

'Bella,' he whispered. 'It's just for a little while. Little more than a day. Don't you think you deserve that? Don't I? Matteo will ensure the club is closed and secure. There's only another hour to go anyway. It will be taken care of.'

He was so high-handed and arrogant and confident. And kind.

'What do you want more?' he asked. 'To

put me in my place or take just a moment for yourself?'

In truth her reluctance wasn't about making him pay, it was about giving herself the time to draw strength to cope with him. He was so overpowering, she couldn't let him tear down every last defence and get a foothold in her heart. She couldn't be that weak over him. But she couldn't say 'no' any more than she could stop breathing.

He smiled. He knew he'd won.

He took her hand. She curled her fingers around his and walked with him. He already had his phone in his other hand and was sending a message, presumably to Matteo.

'We need to go up to the roof.' He led her to the emergency exit door.

'Why?'

It became clear in only a moment.

'You landed a helicopter on the roof of my building?'

'And picked the lock on the door.' He chuckled. 'It was fun. But you need to install a better security alarm'

'It was *crazy*.' She walked up the stairs with him. 'Is it safe to fly at night?'

'I have the best pilot on duty, don't worry,'

Antonio answered. 'And the sun is going to rise soon enough.'

He was right: the sky was lightening.

Suddenly shy, Bella didn't even look at the man in position behind the controls.

'Are we going to Secrete Reale?' It was the smallest island of the San Felipe archipelago, the Princes' private haven. It was the place his brother had taken countless women, if those rumours were to be believed.

'We can't. Eduardo's family is there,' Antonio answered briefly.

She watched as they flew low and fast over the water. It was only a twenty-minute trip and as the sun rose she saw the gleaming white jewel waiting on the water.

Her blood ran cold.

It wasn't a boat. It was a gargantuan palace. From the air she could see the large pool and spa on deck, the surrounding plush furniture scattered with bright white cushions and, on one side, the helipad that they were now descending towards. It was the ultimate example of ostentatious wealth and luxury.

Cold horror slid down her spine as she realised that history was repeating itself in the most tasteless of ways.

She was his mistress and being 'treated' to

a little more than a few stolen hours. Just as her mother had been so many times.

Her nerves jangled but she could say nothing under the noise of the engine. Antonio opened the door as soon as they'd landed and jumped out, turning to help her.

'I can't stay here. I can't be seen on here.' She wrung her hands, anxiously watching as the helicopter lifted off again within seconds of their disembarking.

'If you prefer, you do not have to leave the cabin at all.' He grinned wolfishly.

That humour tore the last of her control.

'You have no idea,' she turned to rage at him. 'How spoilt can you be?' She glared. Wounded and angry with herself for being so weak and willing. 'I don't want to be here with you.'

He visibly recoiled at the venom in her tone. 'I apologise.' His expression shuttered. 'We will return to town immediately.'

She met his gaze. The stiffness in his stance didn't hide the tiredness in his eyes. He was trying to do something nice. He'd just gone about it in princely fashion, arrogant as hell. And he didn't know or he would never have chosen this as their destination.

She sighed and sat down in the nearest seat, literally unable to stand any more. 'Antonio.'

His eyebrow flickered. 'Something you want to tell me?'

She rested her aching head in her hands. 'My mother went on a boat like this once.' More than once. Her mother had loved this kind of lavish holiday. 'With Salvatore Accardi.'

Antonio squatted in front of her so he could see up into her face. She couldn't hide from him.

'They took photos from a helicopter,' she said.

'There will be no helicopters other than the one we just arrived in,' he said.

'You don't understand,' she mumbled, her cheeks scarlet with shame. 'My mother and her lover were photographed on the deck of the boat. It was the moment of my conception.' Or so the papers had speculated at the time. That image—of her mother naked on her back with her married lover between her legs—had been one of the most scandalous images of the decade. The flaunting of an affair that had only hurt all the women involved.

Accardi had denied the dark-haired man in the picture was him.

Deny, deny, deny, was all he ever did.

'I should have talked with you first,' Antonio said quietly. 'I thought you would like it.'

'Anyone normal would,' she admitted. She closed her eyes. 'I'm sorry.'

Here she was on the same kind of symbol of opulence and wealth and corruption, with a man who could have anything—and any*one*—he wanted.

'I'm sorry too.' He caressed her cheek with his thumb. 'But you're not her. And I'm not him.' Standing, he reached forward and scooped her into his arms. 'What we both are is very tired. You've been burning the candle at both ends. You need a rest.'

She half smiled at the stiff way he expressed the old saying. She rested her head on his chest, feeling his heart beating, suddenly unbearably tired. 'Yes.'

'Then let's get you to bed.'

She wanted to touch him and feel the mindless relief that he could bring, but the waves of exhaustion rolling over her were too strong and in his arms she relaxed completely. Her eyes closed as she felt him descend the steps into the body of the boat.

She felt him place her on the soft bed, felt his lips on hers. Too gently. Too briefly. But she couldn't win the fight to open her eyes again.

'Stay,' she murmured, at least she tried to say it but it might have only been a moan.

'I'm right here.'

And he was. Curled up beside her, drawing a soft blanket over them both.

CHAPTER EIGHT

BELLA HAD NO idea what the time was when she woke, but, given light was streaming through the beautiful window, she figured it had to be late in the afternoon.

'I didn't realise you were going to sleep for hours.'

She turned at the sound of Antonio's drawl.

'Hours.' He threw her a mock chagrined look.

With a sleepy smile she rolled onto her back and stretched her toes. 'Sorry.' She glanced back at him. '*Not* sorry.'

Silently he regarded her, his reserved expression more pronounced, when suddenly his solemnity broke and the sexiest smile spread across his face. He crooked his little finger at her. 'Maybe you'd better come here and show me how "not sorry" you are.'

Her body hummed in anticipation, but she

couldn't resist attempting another tease. 'I can't make it all the way over there…' She stretched lazily again.

'Going to make me do all the work?'

'You seem to like to be in charge.' She shrugged, sending him a look from under her lashes.

'You like choosing not to do what I ask.'

'Maybe it's all in the *way* you ask…' She let her voice trail suggestively.

'How should I ask?' he asked. The ominous tone made her tingle all the more.

'With kisses, of course.'

He reached out and grabbed her foot, hauling her down the bed towards him. 'Good thing I know how and where you like to be kissed.'

Bella could only arch up on the bed and let him.

Slowly the sky turned from blue to a burnished gold as the sun seemed to sink into the water.

'Come up on deck,' Antonio invited gently. 'It's almost dark. No one is there to see us.'

He was right, there was no one there. He must employ incredibly diligent and discreet staff—because while she and he had slept, they'd worked hard to create a sheltered lounge area on the deck that had silk walls and sofas surrounding a sensual plunge pool. Silver platters were scattered on the low table, laden with freshly prepared treats. It was private and beautiful and *safe*. She wrapped herself in the robe he'd handed her and curled on the plush cushions. She bit into a strawberry, relishing the burst of flavour.

'Do you often come away on this boat?' she asked, watching in amusement—and unashamed appreciation—as he slipped into the warm splash pool.

'Not as often as I'd like,' he admitted, sweeping his wet hair from his brow and looking too sexy for comfort. 'I usually bring work with me.' He angled his head and eyed her wickedly. 'I guess I brought manual labour with me this time.'

'Manual?' She arched her brows.

He held up his hands, then wiggled his fingers. 'Hours and hours of hard, physical labour.' He sighed theatrically. 'Except you slept away so *many* hours…'

'I woke once or twice,' she informed him primly. 'And found you fast asleep beside me.' He'd been utterly gorgeous too—handsome and relaxed and not at all reserved. 'Admit it,' she dared him. 'It wasn't so bad.'

'I think we both feel better for it.' He rubbed his jaw with a grin.

She certainly felt better. She couldn't stop smiling. The more she was with him, the less she could believe this was real. That quiet, reserved, emotionally distant Prince Antonio was warm and funny and kind when relaxed. When alone with her and away from the rest of the world he was charming and witty. And so gloriously sensual.

It was better than any fantasy. She just had to remember it wasn't for ever.

He'd fallen silent. She realised he was studying her as much as she was studying him but that the laughter in his eyes had faded, replaced by a frown.

'What's wrong?' she asked before thinking better of it.

A shadow flickered in his eyes before he spoke. 'It's weird not to be working.'

She felt certain that wasn't what he'd been thinking, but she didn't challenge him on it. 'You're allowed a break. That's what you told me, remember?'

'You know what it is like to devote your life to your career. It would feel strange to miss a day of training for you, right? It's a calling more than a career.'

'I chose mine. You were born to yours.'

'It's in the blood, I guess.' He reached out to take her foot, rubbing her scarred skin. 'When did you choose ballet?'

'I got my first personal trainer just before I turned two. And a ballet coach.'

His hands stopped the delicious massage. 'A personal trainer when you were *two*?'

She chuckled at his outraged expression. 'I was my mother's cute accessory that she toted around until I grew too big for her to carry.' She'd been the pretty little girl. Until she started to attract comment that she was more attractive than her mother. 'I won a scholarship to study at a dance academy in England when I was ten and eventually she let me go. I loved it. There were no boyfriends, no cameras, no scandal. I could just get on with doing the thing I loved.'

'But you were away from your mother?'

'That wasn't a problem,' she said wryly. Keeping her mother's secrets had been a burden she'd been too young for. And she hadn't liked the vulnerability she'd felt as a teenager with those men around.

He hoisted himself out of the water to sit on the deck and reached for a towel. 'So you weren't close.'

'It was complicated.' Bella frowned. 'I loved her very much, but she had a lot going on in her life.'

'By a lot going on, you mean a lot of men.'

'Yes.' Bella refused to deny it. 'She spent a large part of her life looking for love and she never found it.'

She'd been used and had used lovers herself.

'Are you looking for love?' Antonio asked.

Bella laughed. 'I know what I'm not looking for.' She gazed out at the darkening water. 'Before I went home to Mother for a holiday one summer Matron at school taught me some self-defence moves. Ways to try to get away and a few lines to spin to get some distance if I needed them.'

'Did you need to use them?'

She shrugged. 'Fortunately I spent most of the holidays at other ballet summer schools or camps. I'd only see Mother for long weekends at the most. And when I did, there were lots of cameras. Cameras can actually make things safer.'

He inclined his head questioningly.

'People are more aware of their own behaviour when they know they're being recorded.' She stretched her foot. 'And I think my mother knew there was a safety net in having a boyfriend. It means you're taken.' She smiled. 'It keeps others at a distance. Mostly.'

'But you don't do that too—there's no safe boyfriend?'

'Only the one when I was young and thought I was in love.' She wrinkled her nose at her naïveté.

'But you weren't really in love with him?'

'I wanted to be.' She'd wanted to be loved. To feel secure. To be held and cared for. To be safe. To have someone want her—*all* of her—and just her.

'What happened?'

'I thought he was honest and strong. He wasn't. He let me down.'

'How?'

She didn't like the thundercloud that had appeared on Antonio's face. 'He didn't really want me. He wanted the…fame…of being with me. I was the prize.' She rubbed her arm. 'But he expected more from me. What with my family history…'

'More?'

'A sexpot between the sheets,' she said bitterly. 'Like my siren of a mother. The famous lover of all those powerful men…'

'And you're not a sexpot.' He leant forward and cupped her cheek. 'Not for just anyone.'

She felt her flush rising. 'Don't tease…' she whispered.

He gazed at her, his expression utterly solemn. 'I'm not a sexpot for just anyone either.' And then he smiled.

She laughed a little, as he'd intended her to. 'He was seeing someone else on the side.'

'Because he was a jerk,' Antonio stated simply. 'Not because of anything you did or didn't do.' He reached out and lit one of the candles in the table, casting a small glow in the darkness. 'And since then?'

She shrugged. 'There hasn't been anyone serious.'

'You don't like trading on your sex appeal.'

She paused. 'I don't want to be ungrateful. I know how incredibly lucky I am compared to so many other people—to live on San Felipe, to have secured the financial backing for my business, to have access to all those clothes… some women would love that. But I want to be able to do what I really *want* to do. So all this "show" is only 'til the club becomes a commercial success. I need to earn for a couple of years, then I intend to step back and do something else.'

'But you must love it in part—no one can

fake it for that long. All those photos. All that dancing.'

'I adore dancing.' She leaned forward. 'And I guess I do quite like the clothes.' She chuckled. 'I like feeling like I look okay—it's the way I was raised and old habits die hard—it's a weird paradox. But I don't want that to be *all* I'm known for. When I was dancing, I had that as well.'

'So what is going to replace it?' He looked at her curiously. 'You must have some ideas if it's not the club.'

'No, that's a means to an end. I couldn't get the backing I needed for what I really want to do.' It wasn't going to be a money spinner, but she needed only enough for herself to live on.

'And that is?'

She paused, then laughed at her own self-consciousness. What did it matter if he knew? 'I want to establish my own ballet school. I want to have my own academy and teach.' She felt her flush rising again. 'I know it won't exactly make me a fortune, but it's what I love and I want to share it.'

'You want to teach ballet?' Surprise glinted in his eyes.

'Yes.'

He nodded but then frowned again. 'Why San Felipe? If not to taunt Salvatore?'

'I came for some holidays here with my mother. She had another friend here, for a time.' She knew he'd understand she meant another lover. 'I always loved it here. The beaches are beautiful, the city old and majestic.' She shrugged with a soft smile. 'You know it has a magic about it.'

'And your mother's friend?'

'The relationship didn't last, of course. He passed away a few years ago.' She sighed. 'So there you have it, why I'm here. It's not that exciting at all, you see.'

Silent, he ran his fingers along her scarred shin as if he could somehow smooth it away. 'Why did you never ask for an investigation or press charges?'

'About the glass?' She faltered, but then pressed on. She'd worked hard to reconcile her decision. 'I didn't want them to see how much they'd hurt me. They'd win if they saw that. I'll never let them see how much they got to me,' she said in a low tone, keeping her head high.

'You're not bulletproof,' he said.

'It doesn't matter.' She tried to shrug it off.

'It matters immensely. You had the thing

you love most stolen from you. You were stolen from us—the audience.'

She smiled softly at his support of her. 'It just is what it is. I've accepted it and I'm moving on. I'm a survivor.' She was determined, and proud to be.

The sun had vanished but now the stars had come out to shine. And the moonlight glittered over the water. He fetched one of the blankets that were folded on one of the sofas and brought it back to where she was nestled in the cushions.

He paused at the solitary candle flickering on the low table. 'You want to stay out here with me tonight?'

She nodded and watched him blow the candle out.

The dreadful thing was she'd stay with him wherever he asked, for as long as he wanted. Yes, she was falling for him, but she also agreed because he shouldn't be out here alone.

He'd been on the front page of today's paper, standing in the hospital garden that honoured Alessia. In his midnight-blue suit with his pale, emotionless eyes he'd looked so isolated. She wished he wouldn't shut himself away so completely. She wished he'd open up like this even more. There was a warm, funny, compassionate guy locked away in there and someone—never her—should help him be happy.

He should be happy.

But she wasn't the woman who could make that happen for him. She was the woman who had him only for now.

CHAPTER NINE

SHE WAS WOKEN with a kiss. She smiled—how could she not when he looked at her like that? He was tousled and stubbled and tired about the eyes and so very sexy.

She'd told herself she wasn't going to sleep at all during their night on deck under the stars, but he'd teased her so long and made her come so hard her body had waved the white flag not long before dawn.

'What time is it?' she asked him.

'Stupidly early,' he admitted apologetically. 'But there's something I wanted you to see.'

Holding the soft blanket to her, she sat up on the deck and realised he was in nothing but swimming trunks and a life jacket and was dangling a bikini from his hand.

'You think I'm going to wear that?'

'Or just the life jacket, I don't mind.'

She snatched the bikini from his hand and wriggled into it as he laughed.

The sky was pale blue from the first fingers of sunlight, the ocean still and beautiful and fresh and nothing could mar its beauty. She snuggled against his waist as he rode the jet ski, laughing at his show of speed and control. But he suddenly slowed right down and all but cut the engine. Then she saw what was swimming towards them in a joyous streak of energy.

'Dolphins,' she breathed.

'A whole pod.' He nodded, turning to see her face. 'They're often out this way to feed.'

And *play*. The creatures leapt and somersaulted as if it were the dolphin Olympics.

'There are hundreds of them.' She laughed in delighted awe. She'd never seen anything as beautiful or exhilarating in her life.

'You want to swim with them?' He was smiling at her, looking the most carefree and vital it made her heart flip in her chest.

'Can we?'

'Sing to them,' he said, handing her a dive mask he'd stowed in his vest. 'They'll come check you out.'

'Sing?'

'Anything.' He chuckled at her look.

But she slipped into the water and tried what he suggested. To her amazement three of the curious creatures swiftly circled around and around her. She floated face-down, eyeing the beautiful animals until she had to lift her head and gasp for breath. Antonio surfaced next to her, smiling triumphantly.

'Antonio.' She breathed hard. 'They're amazing.'

'I know.' He hauled himself back onto the jet ski and leaned down to give her a hand. 'You know they're one of the few creatures to mate just for the fun of it?' He chuckled. 'They feed and play and make love all day. Not such a bad life, is it?'

'Not bad at all.'

She watched as he looked out over the beautiful waters again and that carefree expression slowly faded from his eyes. He glanced at her ruefully. 'We'd better get back to the boat. Breakfast will be waiting.'

Their time was almost up.

Back on board, she showered, disappointed when he didn't join her in there. In the bedroom the clothes she'd arrived in were somehow cleaned and pressed and waiting for her. She blushed at the thought of those nameless, invisible servants knowing she was here and no doubt knowing why. She dressed then went to the lounge. Antonio sat at the laden table, already showered and dressed and waiting for her.

'I'll never forget that, thank you so much.' She smiled across at him.

He had been so kind to her, she'd never forget any of it.

For a split second he looked as happy as she felt, but then that reserve smoothed his features and that was when she couldn't hold back any more. She didn't want to see the vibrant man of the night return to that frozen state now they were about to leave.

'You shouldn't be alone,' she said softly.

Antonio carefully put his tumbler of juice back down on the table. 'Pardon?'

'I said, you shouldn't be alone. You should laugh more often. You deserve more happiness in your life.'

His blood iced.

'Do you feel sorry for me?' he asked quietly, but he was so close to the edge of anger.

Last night hadn't lasted long enough. While she'd slept, he'd watched, like some sick stalker. But he'd been unable to rest any more, too conscious of time ticking. And now?

It wasn't a clock but a bomb ticking. He did

not want her to go there with him. He didn't want to hear that lie the world believed. Not from *her* lips. He didn't want her to believe that damn pious story. He was unworthy of her empathy and her generosity. He was unworthy of *her*.

'Of course I do,' she replied simply. 'I'm very sorry you lost her.'

Alessia.

His gut clenched.

'Is that why you're here now, because you pity me?' He stood up from the table and walked away so he couldn't see her face. 'You've been willing to let me do whatever I want with you because you want to make me feel better?'

He heard her small gasp of shock.

'Why are you so angry?' She stood too, following him to the centre of the room, standing defiantly straight and in his face as always. 'I understand you don't want to be hurt again—'

'You understand nothing.' It wasn't about *him* getting hurt. 'It isn't about me. It isn't fair to ask anyone to share the kind of life I lead.'

'That's just an excuse.' She actually rolled her eyes at him. 'Your kind of life can be managed. Media can be managed.'

'Like how that worked out for you and your mother?'

She flinched but the cut didn't stop her. 'Look, I know I'm not the right woman for you, but she's out there. You're just too afraid to find her.'

Hearing her say that infuriated him. Did she really think she was somehow not worthy of him? She had no idea who the worthy one in this room was. It sure as hell wasn't him.

He wanted to shut her up. He should kiss her. Have her. Fast and physical so he could feel the best he'd ever felt in his life for a few minutes again...but he couldn't because she was looking up at him all sincere and sweet and kind and *that* was what wasn't right.

Her eyes were so luminous, so genuine. 'You deserve to find love again.'

No, he didn't. And there was the killer—he'd never found love in the first place.

Bu she misread his silence. 'You do, Antonio. You're a good man. You deserve—'

'I deserve *nothing*,' he snarled in guilt-drenched fury. 'I *destroyed* her.'

Finally Bella was silenced.

And he was aghast at his slip and so, so angry. 'You think you know what happened? You think you know me?'

'Antonio—'

'Stop,' he said, wildly raising his hand. 'Stop and just let me say it. You want the damned, bloody ugly truth?'

For once in his life someone would see him as he really was and it might as well be her. It might as well be the one woman he couldn't stop wanting. And that was good, because she wouldn't want him once she knew. And this would be over.

'I broke up with her before she went away to university. The engagement thing had been more my parents' wish than my own and I was young and didn't want to be tied down. But Alessia was devastated. She begged me not to tell anyone. Wanted to keep it a secret until after she'd gone to England. And we'd let the press know we were no longer together after she'd been there a few months. I agreed. I could see she needed some time to compose herself…' But in his mind he'd been free and he'd been so damned relieved.

'A month or so later I went to see her when Eduardo first went over to study.' He dragged in a desperate breath and carried on fiercely, frantic to get the bitter truth out. 'She'd changed. She'd lost weight and was pale. She was nervy and wanted to get back together.'

He paused again, clenching his fist as he remembered how he'd treated her that day. 'I told her that starving herself wasn't going to win me back. I told her to get a grip on herself and stop the drama-queen crap. I was *so* hard on her.' He'd told her he wasn't in love with her and that that wasn't changing no matter what she did.

He'd thought he was doing the right thing to make her pull herself together. Being cruel to be kind.

It had just been cruel.

He made himself look at Bella, made himself ignore the tears building in her beautiful eyes. 'Apparently she didn't see a doctor until another month or so later. She'd thought the weight loss and sore throat was just anxiety and heartache. Instead it was because of a fast-growing mass in her stomach. The kind of cancer that grows so fast, every day before detection matters. Every day missed meant she was closer to death.'

If found in time, treatment could work well. But if not found in time?

Too late already.

'Antonio—'

'My parents were killed the weekend she got the diagnosis. Her prognosis was dreadful. She decided I had enough to be getting on with, so she didn't tell me. Her parents didn't tell me. Eduardo didn't tell me.'

Because he'd been so arrogant to think he could handle the coronation and transfer of power all on his own. He'd refused to allow Eduardo to return to help. In his own grief for his parents he'd wanted just to *work* his way through it.

But he hadn't realised how much that decision would hurt those around him. And ultimately haunt him too.

'Not long after, I found out through the press, as the world knows. But the world still thought we were engaged…' He released a shuddering, painful breath. 'I saw her once more before she died.' He paused, hating that memory more than any other in his life. 'And the worst of it was, *she* apologised to *me*.'

When he'd been the one to break her. He had never regretted anything as much in all his life.

Bella walked over to him. But he was too on edge and he didn't want her compassion. He didn't want that caring. He didn't want anything from her. Not now. He held up his hand again. Desperate to control his damned emotions. *'Don't touch me.'*

Bella flinched at the raw agony in that command. But this time she was ignoring his rejection of her. She had to. She wrapped her arms around his waist.

'Don't.' This time it was a whisper. 'I don't…'

She held him in the gentlest, smallest of embraces.

'You didn't kill her,' Bella said softly. '*Cancer* killed her.'

'If she'd seen a doctor sooner…if she hadn't been stressed and heartbroken…if she'd fought harder…so many ifs. So many mistakes that were my fault.'

But as he spoke his voice went from emotional to expressionless.

He put his hands on her arms and lifted them so he could step back, free from her. She gazed up into his shadowed face but she could see the determination glinting in his eyes. Goosebumps peppered her skin. He was so used to controlling himself. Even now, he could pull himself together. A cold fear rose within her.

'I will not hurt another person the way I hurt her,' he said softly, intently looking down into her eyes. 'Do you understand?'

'And you think keeping yourself isolated is the way to do that?' It was hard to talk past the giant lump that had formed in her throat. 'You think living only half a life is going to somehow make up for the loss of hers?'

'I lie,' he said harshly, his hold slipping for a second again. 'I live a lie. Every. Damned. Day.' He slammed his fist on the wall behind him. 'I'm not some heartbroken hero. I'm a cold-hearted bastard.'

'You're not that at all.' A tear spilt down her cheek. 'Because you *do* lie. You're protecting her memory. You're caring about her parents and her.'

'It doesn't make it okay,' he said roughly. 'It will *never* make it okay.'

CHAPTER TEN

HE NEVER, EVER should have told her. Because now it *was* pity in her eyes when she looked at him. And he didn't want that. He forced himself to walk away from her. It was over. There was no going back to their lovers-go-lightly affair now.

But she was more beautiful than he'd ever seen her. Her skin glowed, her hair hung in a long, glossy swathe, she smelt of sea and sun and when she'd first got back to the boat after the dolphins she'd looked supremely happy and relaxed. And he was arrogant and egotistical enough to take pleasure in that it was because of something he'd done. But now, the truth was out and she was in tears and their escape was up.

'The helicopter will be here in twenty minutes,' he said formally, determined to recover his equilibrium. 'We have to go back.'

'Of course. I'm ready now.' When he turned back to face her she'd dried her eyes and her back was straight.

He wanted to bring her glow back. That unadulterated happiness that for once had had nothing to do with sex. He wanted to know she was going to be happy *beyond* this moment. He hated the thought of her returning to that club and its exhausting demands. He wanted to know she was going to be happy in her future.

'I want to give you the funds to establish your ballet school,' he said without thinking.

She stared at him fixedly.

'As an investment,' he clarified quickly. 'San Felipe is a cultural capital of Europe and we don't have a ballet school that could train dancers to professional level…' He trailed off as her expression hardened.

'It's a poor investment,' she said. 'You won't get the return that you would for almost anything else.'

He didn't want a damn return on his investment. 'Is that what that backer told you? He doesn't know what you're capable of.'

She would make it a success, he knew, because she would work herself to the bone to ensure she did. She was more determined than anyone he'd ever met.

'I appreciate what you want to do, but I can't accept it.' She was very, very polite.

'Why not?'

She paused, picking her words with care. 'I want to do it myself.'

'You don't have to do everything on your own,' he argued grimly. 'You want the academy, it's yours. No one will ever know where you got the backing from.'

Her eyes flashed fire. 'Are you trying to buy my silence? Are you worried I'm going to go back to shore and suddenly sell my story?' She paced across the room, turning back to berate him in a furious whisper. 'I will never tell a soul what you told me about Alessia. Not a word. Nothing about this trip. Nothing about us. Not *ever*.'

'I never for a second thought you would.' That wasn't why he'd mentioned this at all. He knew he could trust her. She understood too well how it was to be judged.

'I don't want to be dependent on a lover for my lifestyle. I don't want to be my mother.'

'This isn't like that.'

'It's exactly like that,' she snapped back.

He paused as the *whomp-whomp-whomp* sound of the helicopter echoed. The boat's interior had amazing soundproofing, which meant that the helicopter had to have arrived for them to be able to hear it at all. Sure enough, within another second the whirring began to fade as the pilot powered the engine down. They wouldn't leave until Antonio gave the word.

He wasn't ready to do that yet. He walked towards where Bella stood glaring at him. 'I just want to help you.'

'Why? You won't let me help you.'

That was different. This was an easy kind of help. This was just money. 'Bella—'

'I'm not a prostitute, Antonio. I'm not your concubine or courtesan. Don't treat me like one.'

He drew up short, feeling out of his depth now. 'You're a *friend*. Friends help each other.'

'Not like this they don't,' she said. 'We're not friends. And I'm not using you for this, Antonio.'

'You won't be using me.'

Why did she look so wounded? His anger boiled over. He should have known she'd reject his offer. He'd never put himself out for anyone. Never offered another woman what he'd offered her. Couldn't she appreciate that? She was so damn stubborn and independent and now acting as if he'd somehow insulted her?

'Why can't you accept I'm just trying to help you?' he asked.

'Why can't you accept that that kind of help isn't something I can ever be comfortable with?'

'Then pay me back,' he exploded back at her. 'We can make it a loan. Just as you have a loan from the backer of BURN. He's not as nice a guy as I am and yet you're happy to accept his assistance.'

'Ours is a strictly professional relationship. Always has been, always will be.'

'And our relationship?'

'We don't have a relationship. We *can't* have a relationship.'

He knew she was right but her refusal angered him anyway. He loathed being told what he could or couldn't do. 'No?'

'Of course not.' She turned and walked towards the nearest door. 'We need to get on that helicopter. We need to stop this.'

'Stop?' He strode over to her. 'What do you mean "stop"?'

She paused and glared up into his eyes. 'You know exactly what I mean. It was fun while it lasted—'

'You're saying we're over?'

'I think that's for the best, yes.'

'Because I offered to help you?'

'It's really nice you wanted to help, but it's not appropriate.'

'What am I supposed to do?' he asked her in frustration.

'I've never asked you to do anything for me.'

No. She hadn't. And that angered him even more. She didn't want anything from him. Other than hours in his bed.

Which was all he wanted too, right? Because as he'd told her just moments ago, he was never hurting *anyone* the way he had Alessia. Yet here he was, feeling as if he'd just hurt Bella. Badly.

'You're not ending this.' He turned her towards him, then backed her up two paces to the wall. 'This isn't finished. You know it. I know it.'

'Antonio—'

'Shut up and kiss me.'

He needed to vent the frustration rushing along his veins. Sex would help. Sex right now would help a lot. And he knew it would help her too.

'We're supposed to be leaving,' she argued, but her flush deepened.

'I don't care.' He didn't give a damn about

his timetable. He needed her soft in his arms, looking upon him with sparkling, sleepy-eyed pleasure, not this hurt and annoyance.

He didn't want to feel guilt where Bella was concerned. Only pleasure. She'd only brought him a sense of well-being and that was the least he could do for her.

He couldn't make her accept his offer. He, who could make decisions that affected every one of the people in his country with the stroke of a pen, had no power over her. Not even to damn well help her. She would never forgive him for it even if he tried to force her. He couldn't make her do anything—except in this one area.

'In this you won't say no,' he said, aching for her sexual submission. Frustrated despite her warm willingness as he pressed against her. 'You will not deny me the permission to pleasure you. You'll come. Over and over.'

'Egotist.' Her eyelids were heavy but she kept those green jewels tightly focused on him.

'You want it too.' He sighed in gut-wrenching relief when she sighed and turned towards his touch. 'More than anything.' He leaned close. 'Isn't that right? Say yes.'

He needed to hear the words as well as see

the willingness in her eyes and feel the hot softness of her body.

'Only to this,' she whispered back, her lips brushing his as she answered, her gaze still locked on his.

Oh, he knew that. He knew it and he hated it. Her slender body was hot and wet and tight as he pushed his finger into her sweetly slippery curve.

'We're not done,' he promised with another rough kiss as he pressed close.

'I know.'

But they were. And they both knew it. They were both lying now.

'Antonio,' Bella muttered as he pressed tiny little kisses over and over her mouth and his wicked hands tormented her and all the while he watched her. He watched and he *knew*.

Because she'd caught sight of the determination glinting in *his* eyes and knew he made all the rules as he pleased. And he was damn well going to please her now.

And she could no more deny him than she could deny her lungs air. She wanted to embrace him. Wanted him to feel as good as she. She was so hurt for him—more now she knew the truth of his past, than before. The guilt he felt? The burden he carried?

He'd denied it, but he punished himself so much—how could she deny him this last pleasure? How could she deny herself?

But it was too much.

'It wasn't supposed to be like this,' she groaned harshly as he made her come. So quickly. So intensely. And she was so hungry for more.

It was supposed to have only been a physical relief. A one-night stand to boost her sexual confidence, to make her smile, to be her secret. But it had become more. She *wanted* more. But *not* his money. Not his condescension.

And he wouldn't let her in where she really wanted to be. He'd made that clear. This had become too emotional for him. And for her.

Dazed, she leaned back against the wall, watching as he quickly shed his clothes all the while watching her, his ruthless expression so easy to read. He was ready to test her erotic limits again. And heaven help her she wanted him to already. Because that was the thing: she ached to be with him on so many levels—and she wanted to comfort and be comforted by him even if it could only be in this most basic of ways.

'You're sure you're covered?' he roughly asked, pausing just before taking her.

It took her a moment to realise he meant contraception. 'I am,' she assured him. 'But is it too much of a risk for you?'

'Everything about you is a risk.' He pushed her legs further apart and claimed her with a powerful thrust that made them both groan. 'But worth it,' he muttered hotly before kissing her. 'Worth it.'

This one last time.

Their hands locked together, their bodies locked, their gazes locked. He started, a searing, slow, devastating drill. He held her to him, teasing all her most sensitive parts with that skill and determination she'd come to accept was his strength. She couldn't stop herself muttering his name in a broken whisper over and over as he ruthlessly thrust her to that agonising, tense peak.

She didn't want to read all those conflicting emotions in his pale blue eyes. She wanted this to be the carnal affair it had begun as: they were here for orgasms only. Not for opening up emotionally and admitting old hurts that couldn't be healed.

But she couldn't look away, couldn't break the physical bonds shackling her to him. She should. She knew she should. But she couldn't.

Because he held more than her body in his hands now. He held her heart.

And he was about to crush it.

CHAPTER ELEVEN

THE CONJECTURE ABOUT Antonio's twenty-four-hour absence was subdued, thanks to the valiant efforts of Eduardo, who'd surpassed his own legendary ability to charm an entire nation with his smile and good humour. He'd done that by simply bringing his wife and new baby to the event. As it was the first formal photo opportunity with the baby Princess, and was wholly unexpected, the press had a field day. Sure, there were questions about Antonio's whereabouts, but Eduardo had simply told them he was working on an important matter in the palace and had wanted Eduardo and Stella to have their moment.

'It went well. I appreciate your effort.' Antonio stood by the helicopter. Eduardo's wife and daughter were already safely strapped inside.

'There's nothing else you need me to do?' Eduardo asked, his gaze keen. 'I can stay longer…'

Antonio shook his head. 'Go back to the island with your girls. I'm in control here now.'

'You're never not in control,' Eduardo teased, but it was barely a joke.

Thing was, Antonio had never felt less in control. 'Thanks for coming,' he said gruffly.

'Thanks for asking me to.' Eduardo flashed the smile that had made millions swoon. 'See you in a few more weeks.'

The next couple of days passed in a blur of meetings and events, greetings and parties. As they rolled into one Antonio attended on auto. Too much of his mental energy was taken up with trying to forget. Trying not to want more time with her.

Trying not to miss her.

But at every event he couldn't help but cast his eye over the crowd feeling both the dread and hope of seeing her. Bitter disappointment flooded him every time.

But the San Felipe festival fortnight was almost over and his schedule would return to normal busy, not insanely busy. For the most part from now on, he ought to be able to avoid her. He ought to be able to stay in control.

Except the final event loomed tonight. There was no way Bella Sanchez would miss the annual San Felipe Masquerade Ball. Not when she was the nation's club queen. She'd be there in all her sensual beauty.

He buttoned up his starched shirt and fastened his tie. Each guest would hold a delicate mask, but he didn't bother. Everyone knew who he was; there was no escaping it.

He knew there was no escaping that public attention for Bella either. Not yet. But she didn't really want to be in this fishbowl world with a camera in her face every second and the press writing stories about every aspect of her life. She wanted to be free of it and once she'd funded her business she'd retreat into a normal life that had privacy.

That was what she wanted and it was best for her. So she'd been right on the boat: it *had* to be over between them. No more stolen moments. No more kisses. No more laughter. And that was right for him too—he'd had his time.

He gritted his teeth as he fought back the wave of physical longing. God, he missed her.

The only way of getting through tonight was with no *looking*. Tonight he was going to have to avoid her completely.

Bella applied a final dab of mascara. She'd barely been able to eat a thing all day, and now the moment had finally arrived she was tempted to strip out of her glamorous dress and hide at home in her pyjamas.

She'd made a massive mistake in getting involved with Antonio. Why had she ever thought it would only be a simple, sinful moment of pleasure? It had become all-consuming and her heart *ached*. For him and for her. That he blamed himself so bitterly over Alessia's illness? That he isolated himself so completely?

And that he hadn't made any kind of contact with her since they'd left the boat?

Those last few moments together had been so intense, so profound but the memory of them was now so painful. Because despite his imperious argument at the time, it *was* over.

And she was devastated.

But she couldn't let her emotions get the better of her. She had to move forward. She'd long known how it felt not to be wanted or needed or loved, but she'd never let that stop her from doing what she needed to before. She'd go to the ball, hold her head high and continue building that swelling interest in her business. She might not have succeeded in many things in her life, but she was *not* failing at that. She had her gilt-edged invitation card, she had her dress and she had her years of standing on stage and being stared at. This would be easy.

As long as she kept her distance from the Crown Prince.

But when the liveried guards waved her in to the grand ballroom of San Felipe palace an hour later, she stood a second in the doorway and took in the sight before her. There was grand, and there was opulent, and there was majestic. This was more than all those things, but it wasn't the dazzling venue making her dizzy.

It was anticipation and fear and deep-buried desire.

She *ached* to see him.

Her heart thundered as she greeted a few people. Several society faces were now familiar to her and they welcomed her. She knew it was only because of her club's success and her social-media status, but she'd take it.

The first time she saw him, he was only a few yards from her but a crowd separated them. His immaculately tailored tuxedo emphasised his height and proud stance, and she saw he was intently listening to a tall brunette in a form-flattering black gown. Bella froze as she recognised the woman. At that exact moment Francesca Accardi glanced over at her. Time halted as she looked right at Bella, her eyes widening slightly, only then she turned to smile coyly again at Antonio, her face animated.

But she'd offered no nod or smile or any outward sign of recognition towards Bella.

That old rejection stung, but most especially because Francesca was her own blood. Her half-sister was their father's favourite and now she was with Antonio?

Feeling cold, Bella stared at him. He'd turned to see what had caught Francesca's attention. Now his eyes remained on Bella even as Francesca tried to talk with him. But only for a moment. Then he too glanced away as he muttered something in response to the brunette.

There'd been no smile. No polite inclination of his head. No sign of recognition whatsoever. There was only a callous blanking. He'd seen her, but chosen to pretend he hadn't.

He hadn't acknowledged her at all.

Blinking, Bella turned, blindly moving towards the back of the ballroom. She would never, ever let him know just how much he'd hurt her in that moment.

And she would never, ever forgive him.

She spoke to more people. Made herself take a glass of champagne. She'd have a few sips and then she'd leave. But she wouldn't run immediately. She wouldn't give him that satisfaction. So she smiled. Talked. And the hurt morphed into an anger that grew bigger and hotter with every moment. She smiled more. Talked more. Laughed more.

She wouldn't show any of them any weakness.

Ten minutes later she glanced from the group of young businessmen she was talking to to find his fiery gaze on her.

Still no smile. No inclination of his head. But she read *his* anger this time. Adrenalin surged through her blood.

This time she was the one to turn her back.

She kept talking, but her awareness of him was more acute than ever. She sensed him near, looking icy, but she could feel the simmering fury coming towards her in waves.

She sent her own angry vibes right back at him.

As her smile brightened and her laughter rang her tension mounted. He stood nearer still, but still didn't speak. There was only the look, only the sharpness in the atmosphere and only the two of them felt it.

Finally he passed close enough to speak to her.

'You shouldn't be here,' he said in leashed, low tones.

'You're ordering me to leave?'

'As if you would if I did.' He kept walking past her but his quick glance back was rapier-sharp.

She answered with a death look. But her body felt charged. It didn't care whether it was anger or lust, her body just craved his attention. And she had it now—his gaze on her, his eyes watching as she talked with other guests.

For the next half-hour she talked and laughed and acted like the social butterfly she was supposed to be and it came easy. Every few minutes she glanced at him, their gazes clashed, held, *fought* until she turned away.

Still no smile. No nod.

She turned back, registering how crowded the massive ballroom had become. It was filled with people—women—craving time with Crown Prince Antonio. That tipped her tension from anticipation to unbearable.

She didn't want all these others to be here. She wanted to be alone with him. Fiercely, privately, intimately alone. And that wasn't going to happen. This was only a game, only for tonight. She wasn't going to get what she wanted. Not ever.

Her emotions crashed.

She turned, finally ready to leave. She shouldn't have come. She should have proudly kept her distance and encouraged her customers to come to her club earlier.

She'd miscalculated completely. She took the first door out of the ballroom that she could find. So many people, beautifully dressed, lined the corridor, laughing and talking. She brushed past them, following her instinct to get away. She'd got along its length and had just turned right towards the heavy doors when she heard him.

'Bella.'

She paused, but she didn't turn around.

'Second door on the left.'

It was a command. All her antagonism reared in a passion. But despite knowing better, she couldn't resist. She opened the door he'd meant and stalked into the room. It was a comparatively small meeting room—decorated with more gilt-framed paintings and opulent over-stuffed furniture.

He didn't slam the door behind him. But though he closed it quietly, he locked it, then stood with his back to it. Blocking her exit.

'You shouldn't have come here tonight.' He glared at her, all icy-eyed handsome magnificence in that onyx-black suit.

Despite the fact that she completely agreed with him, she wasn't about to admit it. 'You might be the Prince but this isn't some feudal village in the Middle Ages. There's such a thing as freedom of movement and freedom of speech and it's important to me to be here for my business and you *can't* stop me.' She glared at him, unable to hide her hurt or anger. 'You were so rude when I arrived. You didn't even say hello or nod or anything.' It had been the most pointed, painful dismissal of her life.

'You were the one who said it would be best if we kept this discreet,' he argued.

'You were the one who then kidnapped me for a night on your boat.'

'It was still discreet.'

'And hauling me in here is discreet?'

'I didn't haul you in here.'

No. He hadn't. She hadn't felt his hands on her at all.

'So because I didn't speak to you soon enough, you retaliate by parading round the ballroom in that dress.' He gestured wildly at her body.

'What is wrong with this dress?' She tossed her head and glared at him. 'It's a beautiful dress. And, not that it matters, it's a hell of a lot less revealing than the red one I wore at the ballet.' And she hadn't been parading. 'And what would be wrong with speaking to me?'

'I'm trying to protect you.' His teeth snapped. 'Do you really want those headlines—all the "The scandalous dancer and the Prince" stuff? All that rubbish they'll print on endless pages? Your life won't be your own if they find out.'

'I don't need your protection,' she argued. 'You think I don't know how to handle those headlines? You think I haven't been handling them all my life?'

'I didn't want you to have to handle more.'

'No. You just didn't want to acknowledge me at all.' Always she was denied. As if she were somehow shameful. Not good enough.

'I couldn't—' He broke off with a frustrated growl and then stepped closer, his whisper hoarse with absolute exasperation. 'I couldn't bear to even *look* at you because I cannot concentrate on anything else when you are in the room.'

'You're more of a man than that.' She shook her head, even more incensed by that lame excuse. 'You're the head of a country and have had to perform in way more difficult challenges than—'

'All I wanted to do is sneak you somewhere private and—'

'You're not an animal.' And he was hardly all over her now.

Only then he was, standing so close and squeezing her shoulders so she looked up into his face. And what she saw there made her gasp.

'All I wanted to do was sneak you in here so I could strip you bare,' he finished furiously.

The fire in his eyes made her so reckless. 'Then why don't you?'

She bared herself in that one sentence—bringing that desire right into fore.

He smiled. A small mocking smile. 'Always the provocation.' Swiftly he released her shoulders only to bend and pick her up. 'How much proof do you need?'

'All of it,' she demanded roughly as she felt his arms tighten still. 'I need all of it.'

He took three steps to the plump sofa near the wall. She hooked her legs around his waist just before he sat, so she then straddled him. He released her only to grasp her hair and tug so she lifted her chin and met his kiss. Hard and passionate and endless.

She writhed above him, aching to feel him there. Right there. Centring her, anchoring her. Completing her.

Their hands tangled as they sought to touch more intimately. His hands pressed against her curves, teasing, frustrating. She hated her beautiful dress, she wanted to feel his skin on hers. She wanted them both to be naked.

Neither were.

But their passion was utterly bared.

They moved quickly, angrily. He shoved her dress up to her waist with a jerky hand while unfastening his trousers with the other. She lifted herself off him only long enough for him to free his straining erection. And then she gave in again to the delight of rubbing against him. Of fighting to get closer, closer, closer still.

Their eyes met in a moment of frustration and desperation. She felt him move, his hand fisted around the crotch of her panties and he tugged hard. The silk and lace ripped. A moment later she sank onto him—fast and hard and utterly complete.

His hand squeezed her thigh almost painfully. His groan sent a shiver of raw delight down her spine. Now she was happy. Now she was with him. Now time could stop.

But it didn't. It couldn't. Nor could they stop.

He bucked beneath her, powerfully thrusting up, as if he could possibly get deeper within her. Desire for him burned—for more of how good he felt inside her. She pressed down to meet him, wanting more of him. Always more.

They fought to get closer, wild and desperate and so quick yet not quickly enough. And it wasn't slow enough either. She wanted him so much, *all* of him, but she didn't want it to end.

Except it was about to. She felt it coming—that unstoppable wave of pleasure that only he had ever brought forth from her. She arched back, whimpering as he bore it upon her. He thrust faster still until it was a frantic final coupling as frustrating as it was ecstatic.

'One last time,' he commanded. 'I need to see you come one last time.'

She stared at him in blissful agony, then closed her eyes against the despair in his. Bittersweet torture wracked her body as her orgasm hit. It was so good, but it tore her heart. Because this *was* the last time. Her mouth parted, but his hand pressed hard on her lips. In that final moment of release, he silenced her.

'I'm sorry,' he choked as he stiffened beneath her. 'I am so sorry,' he groaned in a harsh whisper as he too hit climax.

Bella dared not open her eyes. She didn't want to face this end. Through the door and walls, she could hear the ball in full swing but the silence between them in the private room was horrendous. She slipped from his knee, turning her back as she adjusted her dress.

'I didn't mean to be rude when you first arrived,' he said quietly, his voice still tinged with infinite regret. 'But I am not able to hide how I feel about you.'

'Is that so terrible?' She braced herself and faced him to ask, 'Would it really be so awful for people to know you'd finally moved on?'

He didn't answer. He didn't have to. Because for once his expression was so easy to read.

To her horror, her eyes filled with tears. He didn't want anyone to know how much he wanted her. Which basically meant he didn't *want* to want her. He didn't want to move on. He *hadn't* moved on.

She turned and ran, just getting to the door and turning the key in the lock. But he must have run too because he reached above her head and pushed hard, so she couldn't open it.

'You're not leaving now,' he said.

'You're not stopping me.'

'I am. This time I am.' He turned her to face him. 'You can't go out there looking like that.'

'Looking like what? A slut?' With no underwear and kiss-swollen lips and the blush of orgasm still on her skin?

'I'm sorry.' He apologised again as he retreated into that damn formal reserve. 'This shouldn't have happened.'

She didn't want him to turn all princely polite. She didn't want him to regret what had happened. She just wanted him to want more the same way she did. But he didn't. She cared more for him than he did her. And she was heartbroken. She looked at the floor, unable to bear looking into that emotionless face of his.

'Forgive me.'

Angered, she lifted her head. '*I'm* not the one who needs to forgive you. *You* need to forgive *yourself*. You're a coward, Antonio De Santis.'

He actually lost colour.

'You think you're so damn noble, burying yourself in duty. You think you're protecting Alessia's name? You're only protecting yourself. You think you can keep yourself safe by not bothering to participate in life?' She shook her head, so angry with him for shutting her out. 'It doesn't work that way. Who's hurting now, Antonio? *Who* is hurting?'

'I'm sorry,' he said tonelessly. 'I cannot be the man you want me to be. I cannot be the man for you.'

It was the most humiliating moment of her life.

And he wouldn't admit that *he* was hurting either. 'I will control myself better in future. This won't happen again.'

'No.' She nodded painfully. 'It won't. I don't expect you to say hello or anything—you're absolved from any duty to be polite to me.' She half laughed bitterly at the heartbreaking mess she was in. He only wanted her for sex, whereas she? She'd gone fully in love. 'This can only be all or nothing. You can't give me *all*. So it has to be nothing.' For her own sanity it had to be nothing. But she was so, so hurt.

He didn't argue with her. 'I can have you escorted discreetly—'

'I'll go out the door I came in.' She straightened and pulled together the last shred of pride that she could. 'But I need five minutes alone first.'

He stared down at her, as if he could somehow break her and make her change her mind. But he couldn't. Her dignity was the one thing she'd leave this room with.

He had the intelligence not to apologise again, though she knew he wanted to. She could see that in his eyes. But she didn't want his pity. What she really wanted was the one thing he couldn't give her. He didn't want to give her.

And that wasn't his fault.

'Leave, Antonio.'

And then he did.

She locked the door again right away and took deep breaths to recover her equilibrium. She was not crying here. She was holding her head high and walking out of there.

No one would ever know how she'd been so crushed.

It took ten minutes before she was ready. Then she unlocked the door, squared her shoulders and walked back down the corridor and around the corner to where the people were thronging and still laughing, oblivious to the cataclysmic encounter in that room so close by. She got into the ballroom and began her trek along the edge to the exit at the end. She was walking so quickly, and with such concentration, she almost crashed into the broad-shouldered man who suddenly stepped in front of her.

'Do you really think you can ever belong here?'

She stared blankly for a second before realising who it was.

Salvatore Accardi. Her father. For the first time in her life he'd addressed her directly. And he wasn't being conciliatory.

Frantically she processed his words, wondering at what he'd meant.

'Look at you,' he snarled. 'You think it isn't obvious what you've been doing?' Salvatore sent her a scathing look. 'Like mother, like daughter. Giving it all to anyone who asks. No doubt you're aiming to get pregnant as quickly as possible and you'll blame it on the nearest wealthy man.' He stepped closer. 'You're the daughter of a whore and you're a whore.'

Oh, God, did he know? Had he seen? She glanced to the side, wondering if everyone here knew. How was that possible?

'You need to leave San Felipe,' Salvatore added.

She couldn't cope with this onslaught right now. Not after Antonio's rejection.

But as she stared at Salvatore, aghast and unable to speak, she saw his eyes widen at something over her shoulder.

'Is there some kind of problem, Salvatore?' Crown Prince Antonio walked up behind her.

Salvatore's expression tightened.

Antonio took her hand, holding it tight. It was the smallest, but most pointed, of gestures and she was so shocked she still could say nothing.

'Bella and I are very close,' he said. 'So I'm glad to see you talking. I'm sure you want to make her welcome. But if you'll excuse us, we're going to dance now.'

Bella gazed at Antonio in utter astonishment. Why had he reappeared? Why had he taken her hand? And what on earth did he mean by dance?

She looked up at him to see, but he wasn't looking at her. He was coolly looking into her father's eyes.

For a single second there was complete stillness in the ballroom. The glittering guests were motionless, all looking at them, like a tableau at the start of an Ancient Greek play—though whether it was to be a tragedy or not was yet to be determined. Even the orchestra was silent. He'd chosen to move in that small gap between pieces.

Then everyone moved at once. Voices heightened, laughter rang. The excitement that had been palpable before was incandescent now.

San Felipe society was on fire.

Salvatore was now the speechless one. Everyone else surrounding her seemed to melt away. And then Antonio walked her away from him, holding her hand as if it were the most everyday thing in the world, when in fact it was the most intimate, most public display imaginable.

'What are you doing?' she asked as he led her through the crowd.

'As I said. I'm making my way to the dance floor.'

She stumbled and he paused, to put his arm around her waist and draw her nearer to him. Her heart thudded. *Why* was he doing this? Why when in private he had just ended *everything*?

He turned to face her and pulled her even closer to dance with him. His hold on her wasn't polite; it was the hold of a man who knew the woman in his arms intimately.

And the whole world was watching.

'Why did you say that to him?' Why tell him they were close? She stared up at Antonio. He was watching her mouth in all the noise—not the way he did when he wanted to kiss her, but with intent concentration. That was when she figured it out. 'You *lip-read* what he said to me.'

He'd heard that abusive 'whore' slur and he'd come running to the rescue.

But Antonio didn't answer her now.

'Antonio,' she prompted him.

She saw the muscle working in his jaw and knew she'd guessed right.

'Can you at least try to dance?' he said shortly. 'People are looking.'

Finally she understood. It was all about the *appearance*. Of course it was.

'You don't have to do this,' she choked.

'Do what?'

'Give me a Cinderella moment so you can control whatever scandal Salvatore might try to unleash. You're trying to protect my name, like what you did with Alessia.' And it was unbearable.

'This is different.' His words were clipped.

'I know.' She felt a blush burn her cheeks. 'This is far less serious. And far less tragic... far less...everything,' she whispered. 'But you're still trying to protect someone, and painting yourself into a corner. This time you don't have to.'

'What do you mean I don't have to?'

'I don't want you feeling obligated to. You've been through that once before and it affected years of your life. I won't be the reason for that happening again.'

'Bella—'

'You know, just because someone cares about you, it doesn't mean you're obligated to return those feelings. You don't owe that person anything.' He owed *her* nothing.

'You're wrong,' he said. 'You are always obligated to do no harm.'

Oh, God, he was trying to protect her. He was trying to be honourable. Even when she already knew he didn't want to be that man for her.

'Okay.' She struggled to keep breathing steadily and not scream at him. 'But you're to do no harm to *yourself* either.' She gave up on attempting to dance. 'This is harming you. This is not what you want.'

He'd just told her so in that private room when he'd promised that mad lust wouldn't happen again and broken her heart in the process. He'd wanted *nothing*, not *all*.

She knew he was protective of those he cared about, or those he felt he owed or who he felt responsible for. She didn't want him doing that for her. She didn't want to trap him into something he didn't really want because he felt *sorry* for her. Not even for a short time.

The tears flooded her eyes and the lump blocked her throat. She could hardly see and she definitely couldn't speak.

'Bella—'

She forced back the burn in her chest. But the overwhelming heartache threatened to drown her. She wrenched her hand from his, turned and ran, forcing her way through the staring crowd, leaving him white-lipped and alone in the middle of the ballroom.

CHAPTER TWELVE

ANTONIO WORKED OUT in the early morning in the palace gym for the first time in days. A couple of times this hour had been Bella's and his whole body ached at the thought of her. Annoyed, he pushed himself harder, choosing to run on the treadmill to cool down instead of his customary walk through the pre-dawn darkened city streets. He both smiled and grimaced as he flicked the switch to increase the pace. No one had dared mention her—or the ball—to him but he'd not thought of anything since.

The look on Accardi's face when Antonio had taken Bella's hand? That naked fury? Antonio had revelled in it. He still did. But his smile faded when he remembered how she'd looked at him in that same moment. And when he'd hurt her so badly.

'Your Highness?' His valet ventured into

the gym apologetically. 'You might need to get ready.'

Antonio glanced at the time and frowned. How had an hour gone by?

He stalked through to the shower. He had only two formal appearances this morning. Once they were done, he'd finally have the time to work out how to manage the intense media and public interest in Bella.

He was still livid that she'd walked out on him at the ball. Never had he met someone so determined to disagree with him and refuse his assistance. Independence was one thing. Pig-headedness another.

What had happened with Alessia was different. She had *died*. It was her parents and her memory he'd been protecting in the aftermath. And, he finally admitted, he'd been protecting himself.

He'd once told Eduardo that he would have married for love. Indeed it was the only thing he *would* marry for. But the way he'd treated Alessia? He couldn't risk doing that to someone else. He couldn't bear the thought of causing more pain and carrying more guilt. He didn't deserve happiness when he'd felt responsible for cutting her life short. He should have encouraged Alessia to seek help; time would have been the best chance she could have had.

But he'd failed her and he'd then chosen work. Bella had been right: it had been the easier option. He'd told himself that the constraints on him and the scrutiny he lived under meant there'd been no chance for love to develop with anyone else.

That had been an excuse too.

But then she'd danced into his life and challenged him on every level, hitting him hard and quick. With lust, certainly, but then there was everything else about her—honesty, strength, humour. She'd made him want to tease and laugh and live.

But in the moment when she'd needed him most, in that private room at the ball, he'd failed her. And when he'd put himself out for her in a way he'd never done for anyone else a few minutes later, she'd then questioned his motives. Of course she had. She'd rejected him. She was *angry* with him.

Well, he was *furious* with himself.

He slung a towel round his waist and stalked to his private music room only to find it now haunted by the memory of her dancing there for him. He sat at the piano and tried not to remember the way she'd straddled him on the stool. But all he could see in his mind's eye instead was the sweetness of her smile as she'd swum and sung with the dolphins.

He'd never felt as content as he had in that moment. Only he'd been too dumb to recognise why that was. And it wasn't about knowing he'd disarmed Accardi at the ball that had made him smile.

It was all about Bella—about making *her* happy.

This wasn't anger he was feeling now. It was *hurt*. He was hurt that she hadn't stayed, that she hadn't wanted him to help her. And it was fear, that maybe she'd hadn't really wanted *him* at all.

Yeah, he was terrified, because he was helplessly, utterly in love with her and he had no idea how to handle it. How could he get her to believe in him? She trusted no one. Now least of all him. And he didn't blame her. He was such an arrogant, ignorant idiot, who'd been so wrapped up in his own self-sacrificing, he'd not realised that he was sacrificing *Bella's* happiness too.

He picked up a phone and sent a message

to his aide to cancel all his appointments for the day.

Because finally he'd figured out that his most important job of all was to love her.

CHAPTER THIRTEEN

NEEDLESS TO SAY the club was more popular than ever. Bella was reduced to barricading herself in her upstairs office. The number of people watching, wanting to get close to her, was terrifying. She was effectively a prisoner but she refused to call on Antonio to help her deal with them. He'd not made contact since she'd left the ball two days ago. It was over.

She'd employed extra security staff at short notice, enforced a strict entry policy and she'd hidden out at the top of the old fire station.

Coming to San Felipe had been a massive mistake. The paradise principality, all beauty and history, with its hint of pirate and sniff of Mediterranean magic, was supposed to have been the scene for her fresh start, but she hadn't even managed a couple of months before monumentally stuffing up by falling in love with the most impossible of men.

It wasn't because he was the Prince of the nation, but because he was so *principled.* He put duty before himself, put the needs of others before his own, and protected others regardless of the price to his own freedom, needs and desires.

She refused to let him do that for her. He didn't love her.

She also refused to give in to her weakest urge and run away. She couldn't. She was locked into the lease. She wasn't going to let the club's backer down. No quitting, no matter what. In a few weeks all the interest in her personal life would die down. The world would think they'd had a fling and that it was now over. Antonio had shaken free of her. And really, that was the truth.

She just had to grit her teeth and put up with the extra intrusion during that time.

But it wasn't that intense public interest that she wanted to run from. It was the heartbreak. She'd truly, totally, fallen for him but while she'd been the object of his lust, the only other emotion she inspired in him was pity. She had his courtesy, his misguided sense of responsibility. And that was almost worse than anything.

Energy—frustration, anger, futility—surged

within her. She kicked the leg of her desk. But heat coursed through her rather than pain—he'd pushed her onto that wide expanse of wood and teased her to her first orgasm.

She didn't want to have it in her office any more. She might have to stay in his city for a couple of years but she didn't need this reminder of his sensual power over her in her home. She'd move the desk out this second. No matter that it was almost midnight and her club was full of patrons. She'd push the wretched thing out onto the landing and get the bar staff to take it away in the morning.

She shoved the paperwork to the floor behind her. Then she tried to shove the thing towards the door. It was so heavy, it took ten minutes to move it even two inches and even then it scraped a deep scratch in the wooden floor and she was furious enough to scream.

'Need some help?'

She jerked upright. Antonio was leaning in the now open doorway, watching with a soft smile curving the edge of his usually firm mouth. He was in jeans and tee, with stubble on his jaw, and his usually impeccable hair looked as if he'd been ruffling it with both hands for two hours. He had dark rings under his eyes as if he'd not slept in days and his pale eyes just burned right through to her vulnerable soul.

He looked *gorgeous.*

Her muscles liquefied. So not what she wanted when she was trying to shift a desk heavier than Stonehenge's largest rock.

'What are you trying to do?' he asked when she failed to respond to his first question.

'What does it look like I'm trying to do?' she answered heatedly. 'I'm moving this desk.'

His eyebrows shot up. 'It looks heavy.'

'Clearly.' She straightened and glared at him. 'And you're in the way.'

She didn't want him here at all—not looking like that. And looking at *her* like that.

It wasn't fair.

'How do you think you're going to get it through the door?' He didn't budge as she fruitlessly tried to move the behemoth another few inches. 'Ask me for help.'

For a split second she gaped. Then she snapped her jaw shut and stood upright to glare at him. 'No.'

He stepped into the room and kicked the door shut behind him. Folding his arms across his chest, he mirrored her defiance.

'Ask me,' he dared, glaring back at her.

Something shifted deep within her when

she saw that flickering expression in his eyes. Something she really didn't want to shift. He couldn't break down her resistance with just that *look*.

'I don't need to move it tonight,' she murmured weakly.

He leaned forward, planting both hands on the desk that stood between them. 'I need to know I can help you,' he said huskily, still pinning her in place with that unwavering, intense gaze. 'That you feel you can count on me. That I'll be there for you.'

Bella breathed gently, trying to stave off the emotion swirling too close to her surface. He still didn't get it, did he?

'I don't want to have to count on you,' she said. 'I don't want to use you in that way.'

She didn't want him to 'rescue' her. She didn't want to be any kind of 'duty' to him. She tore her gaze away, frowning down at the desk.

'It's not using me.' His spread hands snapped into fists, his knuckles whitening. 'I ache for you to need me. Because *I* need *you*.'

Stunned, she glanced back up to his face.

'It's okay to ask for help and it's okay to want to be loved,' he argued roughly. 'That desire doesn't weaken you in any way.'

'Have you been reading self-help memes on the Internet?' she croaked.

'Stop trying to push me away. I'm not going anywhere.' An expression crossed his face—one she hadn't seen in him before. 'I've spent the last two days racking my brains trying to come up with some elaborate way in which I can convince you. Considering what happened at the ball I figured a grand public gesture wasn't it. In the end I decided it comes down to just you and me. No audience. No performance. Just truth.'

At that vulnerable intensity in his eyes, her grip on her emotions slipped. Anguished, she broke. 'What do you want from me?'

'Everything,' he whispered. 'I want everything from you. Everything *with* you.'

'No, you don't.' She shook her head, haunted by all the constraints on them. 'Kings have flings with dancers. They date them. They don't—' She broke off, embarrassed at where she'd been heading. At her *presumption*.

'Don't what—' he smiled a little crookedly '—marry them?' He waggled his eyebrows. 'Isn't it a good thing I'm not a king?'

'You know what I mean,' she mumbled, mortified and unable to think further than her next breath. 'And you're a king in every other way.'

'You think I wouldn't marry you?'

'I think you *can't*.' She burned. He couldn't possibly be serious.

'Have you been reading the papers?' His gaze narrowed. 'You know what they say isn't true.'

'I haven't been reading them,' she answered his lecturing tone scornfully. 'I'm not stupid. I *never* read them. I don't need to read them to know what they say.'

And from his one comment she was glad she hadn't. It had taken sheer willpower and strategic unplugging of the Internet to resist the temptation. But she'd done it. She'd made herself focus on nothing but the club these last two days. She'd caught up on her accounts, her business studies and she'd paced for hours, alone and inconsolable. 'I'm not suitable for you.'

'You're the one declaring that you don't want to be defined by your past, or by the reputation others have foisted on you, yet you're the one saying that you can't be with me because of what others might think,' he said. 'I don't care what they think so why should you?'

'I care about what they say about *you*,' she said fiercely. 'I'm trying to protect *you*.'

'Why?' he shot back at her. 'Because you care about me?'

There was a moment of pulsing silence. In that one moment she was bereft of more than words, but everything.

'This isn't the Dark Ages.' He softened his approach and that wicked smile suddenly flashed across his face. 'There are no scarlet letters in my country. It's not like you have a sex tape.'

'My mother's one is still doing the rounds—' she interrupted, cringing inside.

'And you're not your mother,' he interrupted her back. 'Even if you did, I wouldn't care.' He leaned forward, pressing his fists harder on the desk. 'No more roadblocks. *I* choose *you*, Bella. If my people don't want you as their Crown Princess then I'll abdicate. You're more important to me than anything.'

'You can't do that.'

'I can. And I would. But the truth is I won't have to. Screw the scandal. They'll get over it.'

'No.' There was no way that would happen. 'I don't think so. I think you should leave.' She needed him to go. Now.

His eyes narrowed on her. 'Do you know

what I think?' he asked, bitterness sharpening his soft-spoken words. 'I think that no matter what I do, no matter what I say, I can't win this. You will still say no to me.' He blew out a harsh breath. 'You don't want me enough to fight for this. For us. For me.'

That tore her heart in two.

'Don't,' she begged him. 'Please don't.' Because it wasn't true. It wasn't fair.

She was trying to do what was *right*.

Large tears welled in her eyes, her breathing came uneven and quick and she wanted to run. But there was a huge desk and an immovable man in front of her.

And he wasn't going to let her run.

He watched her for a long moment, seeming to see right through her.

'This is fear,' he told her firmly. 'Pure and simple. You're afraid to believe in me. You're afraid to trust that I'm really here for you, because no one has ever been there for you before.'

Hot tears now scalded her cheeks. She couldn't stop them, couldn't stop him. She couldn't bear to look at him, yet nor could she tear her gaze from his.

'That changes, Bella. Tonight,' he promised

her. 'I'm here for you now. And I have enough fight for the both of us.'

She blinked, spilling more tears, but she still couldn't get her voice to work. She still couldn't get her body to move. She still couldn't get her brain to believe.

'I have been such a coward,' he said quietly. 'I was a pompous jerk, believing that my "duty" was more important than anything when really it was an excuse not to let anyone get close. I have felt so guilty about Alessia and blamed myself for a long time. I felt like I didn't deserve this kind of happiness because of what happened. But you were right that I needed to forgive myself. To move on. And now I think maybe the way to make amends is to love a woman the way *she* deserves to be loved. To love *you* more than life itself.'

Bella closed her eyes, but he kept speaking and she couldn't block him out.

'It's very easy to love someone when she's the right person for you,' he added softly. 'I know you're scared to believe in this. In me. I know you don't trust me. Not yet.'

She wanted to hide because her skin was burning with pain and vulnerability.

'Give me time,' he added. 'We can work on that together, Bella.'

The sincerity in his voice compelled her to look him in the eye again. Hope did more than shift within her, it unfurled.

'You're not just saying this because you feel somehow responsible for me?' she asked. 'Because I'm okay. I'll be okay. I can survive—'

'Well, good for you, but I can't,' he snapped, his smile vanishing. 'I won't be happy without you. And I won't stop until you're at my side.' He growled at her. 'I never understood what love really was until I met you. Be brave. Trust me. Turn to me. Need me the way I need you. Love me the way I love you. Like nothing else matters. Because nothing else does.'

He was too compelling. Too honest. And nothing else did matter except that he was standing miles from her and while she'd heard everything he'd said, she needed to *feel* it too. She needed to experience that certainty in his strong embrace.

He'd fallen silent, watching her process everything, but his smile had returned. She realised he was waiting for her to come to him. Waiting for her to be as brave as he'd asked her to be. And she wanted to be, but her legs trembled as anticipation and ecstatic relief surged through her.

He met her halfway around the stupid desk.

Reaching out, he framed her face with both hands and looked down at her for a long moment.

'Don't you want to kiss me?' She gripped his wrists hard, *dying* at his hesitation.

'More than anything this whole freaking time,' he muttered. 'But I was determined to *talk* to you. I knew you'd say yes if I made love to you first, but I didn't want to seduce you that way. I wanted to be sure you listened. And heard. You need to believe in me.'

He kissed her then—a soft, sweet kiss that breathed love and laughter into her once forlorn heart. Oh, Lord, was it possible to die from happiness?

She rose on tiptoe, refusing to let him pull back too far. She needed him near. She needed his touch. 'You thought you could seduce me into saying yes?'

'I can seduce you into saying anything.' He played up his wicked tease, his eyes dancing. 'Into saying yes, into saying how much you want me…but I wanted you to mean it.'

'Seduce me anyway,' she invited. 'I'll say it. And I'll still mean it.'

'What will you say?'

His question was barely audible, but she read

the hunger in his eyes. Suddenly it was easy to be brave.

'That I love you.'

He too was so very easy to love.

'I do love you,' she repeated, no longer caring that she was crying again.

His kisses smothered her words but she kept on chanting them—in her heart, in her touch. And he met her, promise for promise, kiss for kiss, touch for touch.

He pulled her close. She'd missed him so much. They worked frantically, undoing buttons, pushing fabric aside, eager for skin, sensation, surety.

'No more secrecy,' he muttered. 'No more stolen moments.' He swiftly moved, spinning and lifting her onto the broad desk, his smile both tender and outrageous, his eyes filled with love. She parted her legs and pulled him to her, equally teasing and true.

'Love me,' she begged as he kissed his way down the length of her body and back up again.

'Already do. Always will,' he answered roughly, grabbing her leg and wrapping it higher around his hip so he could rub tantalisingly harder against her core, almost claiming her, but not quite. 'You're mine. I'm yours. Love me back.'

The pleasure was so exquisite she could barely comprehend his words. 'Yes.'

'Keep. Saying. Yes.' He thrust into her with each word, but not all the way, only teasing, arousing her beyond sanity.

'Yes. Yes. Yes.' She never wanted him to stop this torture—but at the same time she wanted it all. Now.

'Marry me,' he demanded as he thrust into her to the hilt.

She gasped and stared up at him, registering the brutally satisfied look on his face as he pinned her hot, willing body with his.

'You bully,' she breathed as she saw the laughing, loving determination within him.

'Not bullying,' he corrected with another devastating thrust. 'Seducing.'

'It's too soon.'

'Always you need convincing,' he teased. But he smiled tenderly at her and gently kissed away the tears falling fresh from her eyes. 'No matter. I'll seduce you every day until you say yes to this. To everything. To me.'

She gasped as he pushed closer still.

He looked into her eyes, his own revealing exquisite torment as he paused. 'We'll get there together, darling. You can count on it.'

He reached down between them to touch

her. Merciless. Relentless. Utterly loving. Determination hardened his face as she trembled, shaking in his arms. There was more than an orgasm coming. There was bliss of the forever kind.

'Yes,' she sobbed. 'Yes, yes, yes.'

EPILOGUE

Two years later

'YOU'RE NOT A good accompanist for my beginner classes,' Bella admonished her laughing husband once the last of her students had left the studio.

'I thought I did pretty well.' Crown Prince Antonio spread his hands in an innocent gesture as he left the piano and sauntered over to where she stood in the middle of the wooden floor.

Bella tried not to be swayed by his gorgeous casual jeans and tee combo but she just loved seeing him this relaxed. 'Breaking into Happy Birthday in the middle of the warm-up was not helpful.'

'But it is your birthday and they loved singing it to you.'

It was his smile that was her undoing—that wickedly tempting glint that flashed from behind that formal reserve and hit her like sensual lightning.

'I've cancelled the rest of your classes for today.' He walked past to lock the studio door and turned back to face her with an arrogant wink.

'You haven't,' she breathed, outraged and delighted at the same time.

Two years in and he was still stealing moments for them alone.

'I have,' he confirmed with zero apology. 'Not only is it your birthday, it's our first wedding anniversary and I'm in charge of all celebrations. Especially the private ones.'

'You do love to be in charge, don't you?' she murmured as he came close enough to kiss.

'I've had a lifetime of experience.' He nodded as he brushed his lips over hers. 'Don't hold it against me.'

Laughing, she curled her arms around his neck and snuggled close. She'd never have thought she could feel so happy and so secure.

Salvatore Accardi had sold his property on San Felipe, loudly declaring he preferred Sardinia. Which was more than fine as far as Bella was concerned because Antonio had been muttering about banishing him from San Felipe for ever on some pretext and that would have only caused scandal and pain, neither of which she was interested in.

Antonio's brother Eduardo had welcomed her with rakish charm and she'd bonded with his wife Stella over her beautiful baby daughter Sapphire.

But the best thing of all was the man in front of her. That her Prince had become so playful still amused her. When the crowds weren't around he was filled with warmth and laughter, but it had spilled over into his public persona as well. The press headlines gushed over the transformation in the Prince—he smiled, he laughed, he was so obviously happy, they seemed to think she was Wonder Woman… So to her absolute amazement, the people of San Felipe had welcomed her completely. Speculation about Princess Bella's possible pregnancy was rife. But that was the one thing she wanted to share with him alone.

She looked up into his beautiful eyes, unable to keep her secret a second longer. 'I have an anniversary present for you.' Even though she was so excited, she was suddenly shy and couldn't get her voice above little more than a whisper.

But he could lip-read and, besides, he knew already, didn't he?

Her eyes filled as he dropped to his knees before her.

'Tell me it's true,' he muttered roughly, wrapping his arms around her legs so tightly she almost toppled.

'I thought we didn't read the papers.' She couldn't resist a final tease as she ruffled his hair gently.

'I haven't read the papers. I've read here.' He placed his hand on the very gentle swell of her stomach. 'And here.' He cupped her breast. 'And here.' He cupped the side of her face, wiping the tear from under her eye with the gentlest finger and then tracing the full curve of her lips. 'So tell me it's true.'

She smiled a watery smile. He groaned, a raw sound of heartfelt longing and wonder. She bent to kiss him quiet, pouring her heart and happiness into it, into him. She could never give him enough—not when he'd given her so much.

'Dance with me,' he whispered against her mouth, pulling her down to the floor with him.

'Any time,' she promised.

Because the music between them played for ever.

* * * * *

In case you missed it,
the first story in Natalie Anderson's
THE THRONE OF SAN FELIPE
series is available now!
THE SECRET THAT SHOCKED
DE SANTIS

WESTERN
WP
PROMISES